WHAT A "GLAMPING" CHRISTMAS IS MADE OF

Star Gazer Inn of Corpus Christi Bay, Book Six

DEBRA CLOPTON

What a "Glamping" Christmas Is Made Of

Copyright © 2022 Debra Clopton Parks

What a "Glamping" Christmas Is Made Of

On the shores of Star Gazer Island and the acres of McIntyre Ranch, love is in the air—it's Christmas, so a-glamping we will go, a-glamping we shall go, down to the seaside…a-glamping all the way!

Yes, Christmas is coming, Alice's second since finding love again and happily watching her sons do the same. Now her number of grandchildren is growing—and yes, once again, love is in the air.

Chef Lilly Holloway's career is doing great since she became the amazing chefs Lisa and Zane Tyson's number-one backup. Her dream is coming true, but something is missing, and she feels it. Now she's sent to help at the McIntyre Camp on the ocean for a favorite group called "A Glamping We Shall Do." These are the campers who helped match up Riley McIntyre and Sophie as they met when she brought the group to his camp. Now they have a baby and are expecting again and need help at the camp. So Lilly is in for an unexpected Christmas adventure—something she needs because she's always lost and alone during the holidays while everyone else is spending time with family.

Abe Bradshaw was a cowboy ranch hand on the McIntyre Ranch. He'd been with them for several years and enjoyed his job. But when Riley and Sophie had needed him at the beachside "glamping camps" to lead the horse riding, he'd had more fun than he'd had in a long time…but most of the women were older single women and never planning to marry, or divorced, or many had lost their husbands and had now found a new way of having fun. But Abe's only thirty-five, and they're far older than he's looking for.

After watching all the McIntyre men find love and looking happy as can be, he's jealous and looking for love is on his mind. So this Christmas, he may spend alone in his ranch cabin. But before that, he's going to have a glamping Christmas on the beach with some of the nicest older women around…and long for a miracle that maybe one of them has brought their daughter along…

Don't miss this trip to Star Gazer Island…as sparkling Christmas lights, soft, white, snowy sand along the pretty blue water, and romance surrounds everyone!

Live, Laugh, Love, and Enjoy Life… It's just too dang short.

CHAPTER ONE

*L*ive, *Laugh, Love, and Enjoy life… It's just too dang short.*

Lilly Holloway smiled as she saw the sign near the entrance of the campgrounds. She parked her small, silver SUV and stared at the cute campground. The camping park was owned by Riley and Sophie McIntyre, and Riley was the son of Alice, the owner of the Star Gazer Inn, where Lilly was the sous chef. Sophie was a wonderful person and had asked Lilly to come out for a talk.

A talk. Lilly really wasn't sure what Sophie had to talk to her about but her curiosity and her devotion to the family had her here.

She had heard so much about this camp but had

never taken time to drive out here and see it for herself. She wouldn't have done it now except this was her boss's daughter-in-law who had asked her to come out. Sophie was expecting her second baby—this one was a Christmas baby. Her sisters-in-law, Lorna and Nina, had given birth to babies Christmas before last, and then Sophie and her other sister-in-law Maggie gave birth in the fall before Christmas. And now Sophie was having her second baby and it was due on Christmas Day and everyone was excited.

Lilly was happy for them and couldn't say no to coming out to see what Sophie wanted to talk to her about. Plus, she'd used this as an excuse to take the afternoon off and come see the camp she'd heard so much about. She hadn't taken time off since she'd stepped in to cover for her two executive chefs, Lisa and Zane Tyson, who had taken some time off for the summer with their now adopted little boy—such a sweet little fella—who had been Zane's nephew's baby. The baby's parents had both died because of a house fire. It had been a horrible thing to happen to a baby, but it was a beautiful sight to see those two chefs, wonderful people, come together—fall in love and make a loving home for little Nicky.

A gush of wishful wanting flowed through her, and she quickly shut it down. She wasn't having a baby; she wasn't even married and was absolutely not looking. She had her mind set on a steady path to her future, and nothing was stopping her this time. One day maybe, but not right now.

Right now, she was acting as the main chef, making sure all the food at Star Gazer Inn was delicious for all who came there, and doing so was a dream come true for Lilly.

She took a breath as the breeze flowed over her, as her gaze took in this beautiful place. There were many spots for campers to park and also an area for tents. Everything was vacant today as this was the camp's day off before the next group came in. That was what Sophie had told her when she'd called and asked her to meet her here. Lilly had actually come a little early and was now glad she'd done that. Her heart pounded a bit as she glanced over toward what looked like a small outdoor eating area, tables with teal-colored umbrellas over the top of them that were not opened but were waiting and ready for the next group of campers. The small building had its windows down, but she envisioned happy campers waiting at those windows for snacks and drinks when they were all here. *Happy campers.* She smiled at the vision and knew from all she'd heard that this was a fact.

Everybody talked about how well the camp was doing, how it was a wonderful place. People enjoyed telling the story of the two founders: Riley, the determined cowboy, and Sophie, a very happy single gal and they met first at a gas station and then here on the first glamping camp on the property. Sophie led the glamping group full of ladies who were mostly age forty and older and called their group *The Glamping We Shall Do* group. Lilly smiled at the name. They were women who were determined to live a fun life, no matter what life had thrown them.

What life had thrown them— Thinking about what life had thrown her set her insides churning. She pushed the thoughts away and focused on the present. Alice had hired Lisa, the head chef, who had then hired Lilly almost instantly to be one of her sous chefs. And this new, wonderful step in Lilly's life had begun. This dream job that was making her lifetime dream of one day becoming a head chef herself, at last, closer to becoming real.

She walked across the camp toward the sand dunes that really looked like high hills, and an unexpected excitement rolled through Lilly. The ocean view was at the top of that dune, and she started up it—she could have taken the trail around, but the hill drew her. She was here; she might as well enjoy it, even if she wasn't sure why Sophie had asked her here today. Smiling, she made her way up the sandy dune, enjoying the moment she topped it—she stopped, breathless from the climb but more from the beauty of the blue waters before her.

She sighed, her shoulders relaxed as the tension that had been building inside of her on the drive out here eased up at the soft blue water and the white waves rolling in at a gentle, soothing pace.

No wonder this camp had become so popular so quickly with "glampers," the ladies who camped together, enjoying the outdoors—sometimes in the woods and sometimes on the beautiful ocean like this. They enjoyed camping, music, and dancing, and they delighted in getting their spa treatments and sumptuous meals, too. It was actually a wonderful idea and even though she had never come out here before, she was glad she was here today.

The water came up to the beach beyond the dunes, eased its way in and then, as if pulling worry, anxiety, and feelings of loss from her, it receded back out toward the open depths, pulling at her as if trying to ease the unrest that Christmas always brought to her.

She was always alone at Christmas—some of it her own fault, some of it had nothing to do with her. It was just the way it was. She had no one but her sweet mother, who was on a well-deserved trip for Christmas. This made Lilly so happy, her mother had put her life on hold for Lilly and now was on an adventure herself. Standing here on the top of the dune, her heart suddenly ached for what she wished she could have—what she thought her mother had finally found while Lilly had been terrible at looking for love. She tried to deny she wanted it—but watching from a distance as everyone around her had been falling in love, there was a longing deep inside that she locked away. Yearning and looking for love had been only trouble for her a few short years ago. And despite the sudden craving for it right now, she wouldn't let it pull her under again. Maybe never again.

Her heart was heavy as she thought about all the wonderful romances going on around her, and that she didn't even date anymore. No, she was fully and totally committed to becoming the best chef she could become. One day she would make it as top chef of a high-rated restaurant, build her name then draw closer to her long-distance dream of opening her own restaurant. That dream ruled over everything that involved her because no one could take it away from her—thus owning her own place was her overall focus.

Falling in love, like everyone around her was doing, wasn't where she was letting her thoughts go. She had dreams and she wouldn't, couldn't let go of them. Her mind stirred up as she breathed in deeply, letting the calming view across those beautiful waters ease her nerves. She stood there, letting the struggle inside of her roll away with each ripple of soft water coming in, then sweeping them back out to sea. Life wasn't something to let sweep in and take over—life was something you chose and worked hard and diligently toward, letting nothing get in the way.

That was her well-learned lesson and not something she would let go of until she reached the top of the dune of her life… This ocean view was a wide-open opportunity, in her mind, of things to come if she just kept focused.

* * *

Abe Bradshaw had watched the beautiful chef get out of her Jeep and survey everything before heading toward the dunes. He'd been inside the large tent where they held the dances and the dinners that everyone loved, and before she saw him, she'd focused on the dunes and walked away before he made it outside to see why she was here.

As far as he knew, she'd never been to the camp. She seemed to hardly go anywhere but home and the kitchen at the Star Gazer Inn, where she was one of the chefs. She was an assistant chef. No, that was the wrong word; sous chef would be the correct word. But he was a cowboy and to him, she was a chef who infatuated him.

Not that she knew it. He worked at the huge McIntyre Ranch and had for several years and loved it. Before that, he'd been a kid in need of someone to care for him, and after being in and out of foster homes, they had sent him to the amazing Sunrise Ranch in West Texas. He loved ranching immediately and found out what real love of a family felt like. He'd also known his life would always be open pastures and ranch life.

Sunrise Ranch and the McIntyre Ranch did business with each other, and he'd helped deliver cattle here to the McIntyre's and knew this was where he was going to live, if given the chance. He'd connected to the McIntyre brothers—Jackson, Dallas, Tucker, and Riley—and when Jackson found out he was looking to start his own life, he'd hired him instantly.

Abe loved it here and knew he could build up his own ranch, but he enjoyed working this enormous ranch, so he'd settled in. Then Riley had opened this camp and asked him to come help the campers who wanted horse rides along the beach. Intrigued, Abe liked the idea; it was a bit like helping a new orphan at Sunrise Ranch ride for the first time. He'd done it many times and knew he could help people ride who'd never done it before. Also, he and Riley got along great, so he'd joined the team when the first group of glampers arrived.

He grinned at the thought of the ladies in that group. They were awesome, and their group's name was Glamping We Shall Do. The words always came out to the sound of music in his head, like a musical chant that always made him chuckle. The ladies—goodness gracious, those ladies were the coolest people.

It was just a group of ladies Riley's wife had been a part of, and she had booked their first time camping here. They glamped at least every six weeks somewhere across Texas and sometimes into other Texas-connecting states. Most of the ladies were fifty and over—sixties being the major makeup of the group. He was about to turn thirty-six years old, so the ladies were at least twenty years older than him, and he adored them.

This year, they were coming two weeks before Christmas and were the last group of campers before the camp closed for the Christmas holidays. It would be cooler than when they came in the summer but not bad—this was the Corpus area, and they were excited to try out this time of year. He was just excited to see them all again. He planned to make sure they had a wonderful time. Especially because he was in charge and didn't want to let Riley and Sophie down by messing up their wonderful record of great camps. They'd trusted him while they were waiting for their second child.

This year, they were having a Christmas baby. His brothers Tucker and Jackson had them with their wives two years ago, and in that time span, Riley and his brother Tucker and their wives had each had a baby so now, Riley and Sophie were adding to the list. He was happy for them and their mother, the nice Alice who owned the Star Gazer Inn, who was one happy grandmother.

Seeing their joy and the love they all had for their kids made him happy. He knew exactly how important a caring, loving family was. He'd started taking on more responsibility here at the camp to enable Riley and Sophie to spend more time with their baby and get ready for their new one. Plus, Riley was taking off because he didn't want to be tangled up with something out here whenever Sophie went into labor. Their little girl was barely walking. Tess was her name, and the little boy they were waiting on was Jess. Tess and Jess—he was betting they'd get those two names mixed up a lot.

He grinned. He'd had a front-row seat, watching them fall in love here at that first camp. He had helped lead all those great glamping ladies on their horse rides, and they had watched the romance too. Now, the ladies were trying to fix him up, thinking they were matchmakers. They'd thought Sophie was too young to be glamping with all of them, but she loved what she did, so they hadn't run her off. Instead, they'd embraced her. But they were all in when they saw she and Riley were meant for each other. Now, they had their eyes on him.

In fact, he liked it; he knew he was ready to fall in love if the right woman came along.

And there stood Lilly. Yep. That beautiful Lilly standing there on that sand dune, her soft dress flowing just below her knees in the ocean wind as her hair danced along her shoulders, caused his heart to thunder.

She was a quiet lady, and she kept that pretty hair pulled back in a clasp when she was cooking. Yes, he had watched from the table he always asked for when he went to eat at the Star Gazer. Everyone who went there to eat outside wanted a good view overlooking the ocean. He always asked for a certain table off to the side with more of a view through the sliding glass doors into the kitchen than a good view of the ocean. He saw the ocean all the time; he only saw Lilly when he ate at Star Gazer Inn.

He enjoyed watching her work—not that he stared the whole time. He hadn't wanted to look obvious or act like a stalker, because he wasn't. Still, he couldn't deny that he enjoyed the view. Her workspace was closest to the door. She cut up vegetables so fast he'd fear for his finger if he tried what she did. And she fixed desserts like they were artwork. He was so infatuated that he went to the inn more often than he should.

And every once in a while, that he knew of, she looked up and caught him watching her. She didn't smile, no, but her lip hitched slightly when he smiled at her—then she looked back down and went back to work.

That hadn't caused him to stop watching her, just more randomly, cautiously, because he didn't want her to think he was a bad guy. And besides that, she hardly ever looked outside those kitchen doors. No, her mind was inside that kitchen area where she made beautiful, wonderful-tasting food. And being so good gave her bosses the ability to take time off this summer while they spent time with their baby boy. That was another tough story that had a happy ending, with them now raising the boy who had lost his parents in a fire. The little fella was well loved.

All the romances and happy endings flowed through his mind as he stood there watching Lilly on top of the dune. His mind whirling, he strode forward toward Lilly Holloway.

Chef Lilly Holloway.

The chef determined to become the best. The fact

that he was attracted to her, like he'd never been attracted to anyone, didn't matter. He was fully aware that it would take a miracle for her to even think about that—nope, romance wasn't on her agenda, and he and everyone knew it.

He pushed all that aside because right now his job was to see what she needed, not to wonder whether he could figure out a way to get her to give him a chance— a chance to at least test whether he had a shot at romance.

That didn't exactly sound right. Give him a shot at his dream—nope, that didn't sound right either. He needed to get his thoughts straight and do his job.

He strode across the sand and made it to the bottom of the large dune where the beautiful lady stood at the top of the hill, her pretty calves directly in his line of vision—*eyes off the legs.*

He yanked his gaze up to her shining hair. "Lilly, can I help you?" he asked, his voice gruffer than he meant to be.

At the sound of his voice, she spun, clearly startled as her gaze met his. Her beautiful hands—the ones that prepared the most delicious meals he'd ever enjoyed—suddenly splayed out to either side of her, as if to flatten against invisible walls.

"Abe," she gasped, lost her balance, dipped backward, and was gone.

One instant she'd been there, looking like an angel, backed by gorgeous sunlight and then she was gone, falling backward, away from him down the other side of the large dune, leaving only a now glaring sunlight with nothing at all inviting about it.

CHAPTER TWO

Abe raced up the sand dune then skidded down the other side, thankful to see Lilly shifting to a sitting position as he jumped down the thick sand hill and landed beside her. Kneeling, he gently touched her arm. "Are you okay?"

Looking flustered and dusted in sand, she lifted her golden eyes to his. "Yes, I think. At least it was sand and not gravel that my clumsiness caused me to fall on."

He smiled; relief rushed through him. "I agree. Here, I'll help get the dust off you." He brushed her shoulders, wanting to run his fingers through her dusty hair but deciding that might not be the right move.

"Thank you." Her lips twitched. "I think I'm fine. That was quite a roll. I don't think I've ever fallen backward down a hill like that before but sand…sand is good."

Those eyes were blinking, and he was glad she didn't have sand on her eyelashes. "Okay, let's see if you can stand up. And I apologize. I didn't mean to startle you when I called your name." He put his arm behind her shoulders, then gently helped her stand.

She gave a small grin. "I should have watched my footing. It's just, in all honesty, I've lived here for two years, I worked really hard to get that job at the restaurant, and I haven't been to the beach yet. I've viewed it from the back gate of the inn on break." She frowned. "But I've not taken time to actually go to the beach. You'd think that if a person lives on a beautiful beach island like this, she would take time to at least walk out to the water's edge. But no, instead I chose to walk out to it here and end up rolling down the sand dune."

He couldn't help it; he laughed. "Today you had your first lesson on dunes, and now we're going to make sure you make it to the camp safely. But first, since you haven't been to the beach, why don't we walk out there and let you see it after we dust the sand off you?" He glanced at her feet and saw she had sandals on, but they were a little dressier than a beach sandal—climbing up the dune had been hard too, unless the small hill had helped. Now, he met her gaze just as she glanced down then back up at him.

"I don't think these are going to walk out there, although they were little picks that helped me up the hill," she said, as if reading his mind. "That's much better, don't you think?" She finished dusting off her knees and her legs, and the motion drew his eyes to her pretty legs.

He yanked his gaze back up and smiled at her. *Goodness, she was beautiful.* "So, do you want to go for that quick walk? I know you must be here for something, but it's just right there."

He hoped she would go for the walk but also wanted to know why she was here. It was highly unusual; as far as he knew, the woman worked most of the time. She was a very aggressive chef who would soon undoubtedly be the chef of her own place or the number-one chef wherever she chose to go. He knew she wouldn't be at Star Gazer Inn as a sous chef forever, considering both Zane and Lisa were simply taking some time off but would be back at work soon.

"I'll do that." Her soft voice floated on the wind and slammed him back to earth as she placed her hand on his arm.

A shock wave blasted through him—she was simply using his arm to steady herself as she lifted her foot and slipped off a shoe and then repeated the action. Then, with the dressy sandals dangling from her fingertips, she straightened back up and met his gaze. He hoped his expression didn't show the jolt of a simple touch of her hand had sent through him.

Wow, this was a first for him. He'd never, ever reacted like this to a woman's touch...*and she had known his name*.

* * *

Lilly's fingers tingled when she'd grabbed hold of Abe's arm for support. She quickly got her shoes off and then stood on her own. At least, she hoped she'd stand on her own and not roll around on the ground anymore. This cowboy always made her feel unstable, and the moment she'd heard the sound of him calling her name, she'd reacted by spinning around too quickly and then laying face-first in the sand.

Thankfully, she'd scrambled to a sitting position and had made sure her dress was in place. How embarrassing it would have been if he'd found her sprawled very unladylike there in the sand. This was the one man she had known she might see when she came out to the camp, and the one man she didn't want to see—well, she did but she didn't.

This was the one man who came to the inn for dinner and the one man who made her nerves act up like they never had where cooking was concerned. Yes, they acted up *out* of the kitchen, but the kitchen was the one place she normally had everything under control. Except when Abe was sitting at the corner table on the patio.

He came to the inn about once a week to eat. Yes, she'd noticed—hadn't even known his name until Alice, the owner of the inn, had been standing beside her admiring a dessert Lilly was making, then spotted Abe through the window and gone to say hello. Later, after giving the cowboy a hug and talking for a few moments, she'd come back inside and, for some reason, told Lilly what a great young man Abe was and that as far as she knew, he wasn't dating anyone.

Why had Alice told Lilly that? She also didn't know why Alice told her that he was her son, Riley's, right-hand man at the camp.

Now, it slammed into her that he was probably wondering how she knew his name.

Despite not wanting to she'd listened for his name after he'd talked to Lisa and Alice one day and they'd discussed what a great man he was after he left. She'd found herself watching for him, the great man, to come to the inn for lunch or dinner. Watching his table—as her mind had labeled that table for two. If he showed up, her concentration wavered from where it needed to be—on the food she was preparing—and her food creation became a bit off. Not something she wanted at all to happen.

So, she strove to keep her eyes from staring because

once, their gazes had locked; in that moment, his lips had lifted into a smile. She'd paused, looked down and made certain not to look that direction again. Thankfully, when she carried her creation to join the chef's meal going out, she could see from an angle whether he was still there and made sure when she was at her work table, no more accidental eye connections were made. She had to be the best at what she did, and there was no way she was letting a distracting male ever get in the way again.

Even if he seemed to be a very nice man and, of course, Alice, her boss, had hugged him and said he was great. Now, the cowboy who intrigued her stood before her, had helped her get up out of the sand, and she was, at the moment, at a loss for words. Her fingers still tingled from touching his muscled arm, and she was staring into his amazing emerald eyes.

Speak, Lilly—speak and don't go for a walk with him. "Actually, I'm, I'm Lilly Holloway, from the inn."

He grinned. "I know. I'm a great fan, and I'm Abe Bradshaw. I enjoy your cooking."

Her heart rattled and her hand shook. "Yes, I've

seen you there a few times. Lisa and Zane are fantastic chefs."

"And so are you. I've been there when you're filling in for them."

His words tickled her insides and made her breathless. "Good," she managed, and more words didn't come.

"So, you're here for something?" he asked, helping her out.

"Yes," she practically gasped, so anxious to have something to grab hold of. "I'm meeting Sophie here, and I don't want to keep her waiting if she shows up while we're walking on the beach, so I better head back that way."

He crossed his arms and nodded slightly, as if getting it finally. "You're meeting Sophie." He grinned widely, and she wondered why. "That's great. So, let's get you back to the tent. If she told you to be out here, then she'll be here too." He started to walk, and Lilly did too as he glanced at her. "They are really ready for their new baby to join the family, so it's taking them away from camp for a little while."

"Yes, Alice is excited too. But I don't have the slightest idea what Sophie wants to see me about."

Lilly liked how Abe took what she said and didn't act as if she were irritating him for not going for a walk as he'd suggested. There had been a time when she'd let men—more than one—be the ones with all the right ideas. She'd let their ideas steal her dreams away. Three times—*three.*

She'd given her dreams away because she'd had a heart that was too easily swayed and felt her dreams were less important than theirs. She'd let each one take her thoughts away from her goals, and then all of them had broken that feeble heart and left her with nothing.

Three lousy times she'd let her career plans be kicked to the side, her heart damaged, and her self-esteem beaten down. But not anymore.

Now she thought *only* of her goals and was finally on target to be the chef she'd always dreamed of becoming. What her sweet mother had dreamed of her achieving. That goal now took all of her time, and letting someone play with her heart had no place in her life. She'd kicked the mistakes of making wrong moves to the sideline—kicked it so *hard* to the sideline that wrong moves had nosedived deep into the dirt.

She had vowed to herself never again would anything or anyone get in the way of her goals. She loved her life now and as she looked into Abe's amazing emerald eyes, she smiled but held firm. "Thank you, but Sophie asked me to meet her here at the camp. She has something to talk to me about, so I need to go back and wait."

He cocked his chin slightly and his lips curved up at the edges. It was a thoughtful, slow grin, and it instantly set him apart from every other good-looking man and drew her attention—which irritated her. She didn't want to be drawn to him, but she was.

He waved his hand, motioning toward the trail, not the dune. "Then let's go."

He took a step and as she started to walk, he fell into step beside her. She was carrying her sandals in one hand, and they were between them; at least something was as her mind locked up on that slow grin. No, she stuffed thoughts of the grin away, tucked them behind the closet door of her brain. Because her *brain* was what she let lead her now, *not* her wimpy heart.

And she was determined to not waver.

He gave her a sideways glance. "So you really don't have any idea why Sophie wants to see you out here?"

"No, I'm clueless. She just asked me to come out. I'm working most of the hours now while Lisa and Zane take time off with their baby, and it's been a lot of hours—I've loved it, so no complaining from me. I just want to make sure I don't let them down while they're having family time off, so I've been really concentrating on work. But, coming out here was too tempting to pass up, and Sophie sounded really excited about seeing me. So here I am."

"I see," he said, his tone thoughtful.

She found his response a bit odd. "Do you know something?"

"No, just asking."

They emerged from the sand dunes on the trail, and she spotted Sophie's SUV coming down the drive. Relief raced through her. "Looks like I'm about to find out. So, thank you for coming after me and walking me back." She had time as Sophie wasn't yet parked.

"You're out here getting ready for campers for the coming week?" Her curiosity got the better of her. He grinned.

Oh goodness, that grin…

"I am getting ready for my favorite group—the older ladies. Sophie used to be in their group. It's called the Glamping We Shall Do group. But they are wonderful women, and I always look forward to seeing them. And I want to be especially ready for them since it's Christmas."

She loved his sincerity. "If you take care of them like you took care of me, then you'll do a great job."

"Thank you very much. I'm just glad I was there, and sorry I startled you and caused your fall."

"I probably would have fallen anyway, so don't take the blame, please." She meant it and was glad to see a hitch of his lip as they reached Sophie. She pulled her gaze from him and focused on the reason she'd come here.

"Hi," Sophie greeted them as she closed her SUV's door.

"Hey, boss lady." Abe grinned. "We went for a

little walk over the hill there so Lilly could see the view. Now, she's all yours. I'll head back and finish setting up for our favorite group of glampers."

Sophie smiled, her eyes sparkling, and she placed her hand on her humongous pregnant stomach. "Thank you so much, Abe. We couldn't do without you." Her smile switched from him to Lilly. "Isn't he the sweetest cowboy?"

Lilly's gaze instantly went from Sophie to the topic of conversation. Her breath caught as his humor-lit eyes met hers. She couldn't lie as he grinned. "He's great," she said, and at her words, he tipped his hat then turned and strode toward the tent. Her gaze stuck on him, watching the way his lean hips moved in rhythm with his strong shoulders.

"He's a cutie, isn't he?"

Sophie's words cut into her hijacked brain, and Lilly yanked her eyes off where they shouldn't be and met Sophie's all-seeing gaze. She clearly saw what Lilly hadn't wanted anyone to see—her interest in Abe. "He's very nice," she forced out firmly.

Sophie chuckled. "A great guy, handsome, very

dependable, and hard-working. No bad things about him that I know of."

Lilly's brows cinched up as she stood there. "I've gotten that impression. So, what did you need to talk to me about?" She needed to get this conversation on anything other than Abe.

* * *

Abe smiled as he left the ladies to talk. He strode to the large tent, glad he'd kept Lilly's fall to himself. He was extremely thankful he'd been there to help her, but, if she wanted to tell anyone about the fall, that was her choice.

Now, after leaving them to talk, his focus was on what they were discussing. Not that it should be. He paused in the center of the building and scanned the area. This was where the music and dancing happened. Where the catered dinners were served, and where the ladies visited and danced—which was great because these ladies not only loved camping, they loved dancing.

They danced as a group, determined to live a life they enjoyed, many seeking to find a new life after losing the husbands they'd loved; some, after divorce, and others who had never been married or found love or even looked for it, were here to simply enjoy life. He liked their determination to live a life *they* loved. Even though for many it meant doing the things they'd always enjoyed before with a mate, but now with women who had been through similar tough times.

Thus, this group had been formed by Sophie, the young woman who'd just wanted to enjoy life in her own way. Together, they'd traveled and enjoyed the outdoors. He smiled, thinking about the fun they were going to have this week. He would make sure they danced, got to talk, laugh, and sing all they wanted. And starting the first day after their arrival, they'd get to ride horses, and get manicures, pedicures, and all kinds of spa treatments, including massages. There would be a lot going on and, of course, they'd always get the chance to watch the sun set over the beautiful water or, if they were early risers, to watch the sun peek up over the horizon.

He was in charge of camp this time, while Riley stayed home with his sweet wife and son, waiting on their new baby. Abe was making sure everything was clean and ready, and he hoped his hunch was right. He hoped the reason Lilly was here was because they were going to invite her to fill in for Sophie while she waited on her baby's arrival.

He liked that idea. Lilly would be perfect for this exceptionally fun camp week, and all the wonderful women would love her. This extraordinary group of ladies would need a special lady to help make sure all their needs were met. Something he might not be able to do because he was a man and would be busy making sure everything ran smoothly.

After this last camp of the year finished, the camp would be closed for three weeks for Christmas and New Year's Eve. This meant he would be at the ranch working like normal and alone in his cabin on Christmas Day. So, for him, this week was his Christmas.

The McIntyres always invited him to come eat and celebrate with them on Christmas Day at the main house, but he wouldn't do that. He wanted them to be at home with their wives and kids, enjoying the special time with their families—he understood how important that was. He'd learned that at the foster ranch he called home.

He could go there but hadn't planned to do it this year. He'd agreed to work during the Christmas time while many of the cowboy hands spent time with their families. As he stood there thinking about that, his thoughts swung back to the beautiful lady standing out in the Corpus Christi area Christmas weather right now. Not that he was worried; it was about seventy degrees today, exactly what he liked. Until she'd toppled off the sand dune, Lilly looked as if she loved this weather too.

He hoped she took the job. If he was right, and he had a huge feeling that was what the conversation was about. He hoped it was.

If Lilly Holloway took the job, *that* would make Abe Bradshaw's first Christmas wish in years and years come true.

CHAPTER THREE

Lilly stared at Sophie as they walked, still not completely getting the realization that Sophie was telling her that Zane and Lisa were coming back to the restaurant.

Her head spinning, she kept walking toward the beach—by the path, not the dune. No more rolling down the dunes for her. And with what she was hearing, it could easily have happened if they'd been standing up top.

She halted as the beach came into view and faced Sophie. "I'm confused—why are you telling me this? I've always known they're coming back. I'm just filling in for them. You are the one telling me and not them…is something wrong? They're my bosses." Her heart slammed against her lungs, making breathing a bit tough.

Had she not done a good enough job that they had to get someone else and let her go? Odd as it sounded, it was what was rolling through her tangled mind. Business at the inn had been wonderful, if being packed was a hint. People had complimented her food so much—*was that why?* That didn't seem right. She was supposed to copy Zane's and Lisa's cooking, and she had done that. True, every once in a while, she'd added a little twist to a recipe, but it had always gotten good comments.

Was that it—*was that what she'd done wrong?*

Sophie placed a hand on her forearm. "Believe me, you've done nothing wrong. You've been amazing. I just asked them if I could tell you they were coming back because I wanted to ask you something important. Also, I figured you might need a little time off after how hard you worked filling in for them. They agree wholeheartedly."

She was *totally* confused now. "What do you need to ask me?"

"Want to ask you." Sophie smiled. "Truth is, I need *you.* Would you please give me a week and a half of your coming two weeks of vacation for having worked so hard? That's what they're giving you…three, if you need it. But I only need one and a half weeks of it. They're coming back the day after tomorrow, and I was wondering, since you've had no time off and now they'd give you as much as you need—anyway, I need you here. They're coming this week, for the last camp before the Christmas holidays. It's the last camp before we reopen after New Year's Eve."

Lilly's head was still spinning; words weren't part of it.

Sophie smiled and placed her hand on her stomach. "I'm going to be out with the baby, and my special group of ladies are coming to camp before the holidays. That great guy who walked with you out to the beach a while ago will be in charge, taking Riley's place. He's got the ranch hands lined up to take everyone horseback riding instead of him, since he'll be overseeing everything like Riley normally does."

"But I don't understand." This was so *not* her.

Surely, she was hearing it wrong.

"The food is all taken care of, brought in by restaurants from all over, so no cooking. But the wonderful ladies, my buddies, need someone making them feel welcome, just helping them have a great time. That's what I've always done. I can tell you, Connie, Ida, and Maggie are going to run the show, so no stressing out over that. They always help me. You're going to love them, and they're going to love you too. So, if you take my offer and give them a chance, I would love it. And I promise you, your pay will be absolutely fabulous, but what you get from it will be even more wonderful. Believe me, I get rewarded every day when we hold a camp out here. But when my gals are out here, the gals I traveled with all over Texas, it's amazing—"

"Are you asking me to take your place?" Shock filled her, so she repeated what she knew was being asked. This couldn't be.

"You'll love it. I used to travel once a month or every six weeks with these ladies, so I know firsthand how amazing they are. For a gal who never planned to get married, I was pretty young to be hanging with all the divorcées and the sweet ladies who lost the loves of their lives. And the ones who never got married like me but loved camping. So, I was surprised when I met Riley here, met *my guy*. My heart sings that song every time I think of him. They'll probably play it like they always do, and you can get out there and dance with them… So, what do you think?"

Think? Her mind spun; her head was not focused. Sophie had been talking fast. It was clear she loved this group of ladies and Riley, too, but what wasn't clear was what she was asking Lilly. *She wanted her to come here and help hold a camp?*

Lilly had never been camping in her life, much less this new glamping everyone talked about.

She didn't go to spas, which she knew was one of the many things they did here for these glamping ladies. They had spas, manicures, pedicures, and massages. Oil baths, she'd heard. Lilly had never even done *any* of those things. She had just concentrated on not messing up anymore.

She'd concentrated on finally fulfilling her dream of becoming a chef. And she was almost there; right now she was sous chef, second in line to Lisa and Zane. They both well-deserved their titles, and had made an unbelievable reputation together at the inn.

And they'd blessed her when they hired her and trusted her to fill in for them.

The reputation that those two chefs had, and now being on her résumé, was unbelievable. She'd already gotten offers from other restaurants to become their head chef just because they'd heard she worked under Lisa and Zane. But she didn't believe she was ready, but she had a few restaurants on her list that she planned to apply to when she felt she was ready.

Now she was being offered overseeing a glamping camp.

Alarm rang through her as she fought to keep her expression from showing the pure distress taking over. She had to say something. *Speak!* "Well, I know you both have a wonderful time out here. B-but I love what I do. Being a *chef* is what I love, and overseeing a group of ladies and helping them relax and, um…have fun," she faltered as her thoughts dropped to the ground. *Had that sounded as wild and crazy as she felt?*

Sophie grinned and her eyes danced. "Whoa, whoa, slow down. Yes, it may sound like an odd thing to ask you, the wonderful chef that you are, and you really, *really* are amazing. I'm telling you, Zane and Lisa are thrilled about how you handled the inn for them. This is not, I guarantee you, not a downplay of any sort. This is something that we all agree and think can give you another wonderful asset for your resume. We all know you'll soon be looking for your next step up into the wonderful world of being the executive chef of a very fortunate restaurant. We all know you're amazing, and wherever you choose will be lucky to get you."

Again, Lilly couldn't find words. Words weren't her strong point, but she was so overwhelmed by Sophie's praise and her brilliant smile. "I don't know what to say—"

"No worries. Don't think we don't know that you, Lilly, are amazing. And that's why you are the one I'm asking to take my place, because what you feel there in that restaurant, making those incredible meals, is what I feel around these wonderful ladies who are going to be here this week. They're my people, and I think you would love them. I know they're going to love you, so if you could do me this huge favor I would be forever grateful. And I'm thinking it would be good for you to take time off from the kitchen.

"Maybe just enjoy time with the ladies while getting out from behind the stove would be good for you. If you interact with people more, it could elevate you behind that counter and grill. Does that make sense?"

Lilly's heart thundered, banging in her ears as she stared into those beautiful eyes of Sophie's. Her words spoke to Lilly in a way she'd never expected. She wanted to be the best chef there was, yes; it was a huge dream but in her heart of hearts, she wanted it. It was all she wanted to be, and she felt like maybe seeing the world a little differently from another point of view like Sophie was suggesting might be a good thing. Because yes, she lived in the kitchen.

They'd made it across the sand and now she stared out over the beautiful water as the soft waves rolled in. Her thoughts reeled; she hadn't walked on the beach even though she lived near it. She hadn't ridden a horse on the beach, and she always wanted to. And there was also a cowboy standing in that big tent up there who knew how to do that—not that she wanted anything else to do with him other than learn to ride a horse.

It was just a week and a half.

She had worked really, *really* hard to make sure everything was perfect while Lisa and Zane were out with that sweet boy of theirs. Suddenly, as a gush of wind blew in, her dress feathered out, dancing around her knees and across her face, lifting strands of her hair as the feeling of want filled her. Maybe trying this was what she needed.

Glamping. She almost laughed as she looked at a smiling Sophie. "You are an extremely good saleswoman. It sounds like a lot of fun and honestly, because I was so against it, I was shutting it out. I've shut so much out as I've tried to achieve my goals. Maybe it's the perfect timing for me to step out a little."

"Bingo!" Sophie grabbed her up in a hug—her baby belly between them but still a hug. "Thank you. You're going to *love* it, and my gals are going to love you. They're wonderful. And," she leaned back, grinning,

"I'm not saying anything more than this about that amazing cowboy who'll be running the show except that he's wonderful. He'll help you in any way you need him, so don't be afraid to ask. Now, I'll call Lisa and Zane and tell them the exciting news that you're taking me up on this offer. They'll come into the kitchen tomorrow and see you and y'all get everything straight for your time off. Then you can come out the next day, and Abe will help you get the drift of what you'll be doing."

"That quickly?"

"Yes. Honestly, I do really need time off. Just standing here for this short time, I'm already feeling heavy and tired. My darling baby is truly growing and you're doing us a huge favor." She chuckled, then grinned. "You're doing a *huge* favor for a *huge, excited* lady. We have a lovely camping trailer for you to stay in and it's near Abe in case you need anything. Again, Abe is wonderful and will show you everything, but if you need anything, call me. I'm only a phone call away—well, until the baby comes. Then I might be a little harder to get ahold of. But we're there for you, and

I just can't tell you how grateful I am because I know with you and Abe, my ladies are going to be in the best of hands."

Lilly took in all of Sophie's excited words and, inside, she was trembling but smiling too. This could be an adventure.

When was the last time she'd had an adventure that didn't have to do with food? Although she loved food with all her heart, she'd heard everyone talking about those sweet glamping ladies, and she was ready to meet them.

She was more than ready to meet them; she actually couldn't wait.

CHAPTER FOUR

be watched from inside the large tent. Curiosity and yep, attraction was driving him as he watched Lilly and Sophie walking back from their talk. They stopped at Sophie's SUV and as Sophie leaned in and gave Lilly a hug, he knew what he'd thought was happening was true. She'd asked Lilly to help him hold this next camp, and from the soft look on Lilly's pretty face, he knew she had agreed.

And that made his heart go berserk.

They would be working together for the next week and a half. Maybe this was his chance to get to know her better. To get her to notice him—she had been on his mind for a while now.

He wasn't one to look to the future much. He

concentrated on making the best out of each day. That helped ensure he had good memories. His father had abandoned him and his mom early. The man had been rough when he'd been around, and Abe hadn't missed him. His mom, however, had struggled, while he was there and after he'd left. She'd come down with a lonely heart, turned to drinking, and Abe had been taken away. He'd been thirteen, angry at life and both his parents. He tried to help his mom, but he had failed her and lived with that every day. Despite being a kid, he'd taken it personal that she had gone down that dark road and he hadn't been able to help her.

He was put into foster care and hadn't done well in the homes they had sent him to. It wasn't their fault; he was too angry to let anyone help him. Then his care worker sent him to Dew Drop, Texas, to the foster ranch there. And there at Sunrise Ranch, he had become a cowboy.

He had great, deep memories there despite having a hurting heart from his terrible life and loss. Sunrise Ranch had become his home. The three brothers' whose mother had dreamed of making their enormous ranch into a home for boys with hurting hearts like his, they'd lost her before her dream came true. They'd had hurting hearts too, from a different side. They'd been loved deeply and cherished. But when their dad and grandmother made her dream come true, Abe's place of belonging had been found. Morgan, Rowdy, and Tucker had become his brothers, their sweet mother his guardian angel, and their dad and grandmother his path to a foundation of love and strength.

They had all been through hurting hearts since they lost their mother. Lydia McDermott lost her battle with cancer before her dream was anything but a dream. But although they were all hurting, their dad, Randolph, and his mother had brought to life her dream of opening a home for boys who hadn't been loved as much as she loved her boys. He had been one of them. Many of the boys who were sent there had gone through horrible traumas far worse than his, and Sunrise Ranch had been their miracle.

All those boys were now his brothers and soon he'd be heading south to the yearly family reunion there in Dew Drop, Texas. That special town held a fantastic reunion every year, and he always looked forward to it. But Christmas wasn't a time he went back. He let the brothers with families enjoy their time with their wives and kids, and he didn't go as a sidekick despite being asked every year.

That wasn't a part he'd taken up with yet. He hadn't wanted to take on the fear that some of his father's bad habits could have worn off on him… He yanked his hat off, tapped it on his knee and ran his free hand through his hair as awful thoughts, questions if somehow he took after his biological father, filled him. *What if—*

He wasn't going there.

He didn't feel deep down inside he could be like that, and he'd seen many of his brothers marry and live happy lives. But he'd never felt the draw to bring himself to that moment in time.

That moment when he risked his heart.

Yes, he'd learned to be strong on the McDermott Ranch among his brothers and from the townsfolk of Dew Drop, Texas, the wonderful town full of ladies who had helped him and helped all the boys who called the ranch home.

The amazing people of Star Gazer Island reminded him of Dew Drop in many ways, which in his eyes was the hugest compliment he could give anyone. While brothers Riley, Tucker, Jackson, and Dallas ran the McIntyre Ranch like Morgan, Rowdy, and Tucker—another connection the families each having a brother named Tucker—ran the McDermott Ranch, both done so with love and devotion and now they were his connection in this place he had chosen to build his future.

He had watched each of the brothers of both families marry and only now was he thinking that he might be ready to look to his own future in that way. It had been seeping into him little by little over the last year though he'd not let himself think much about it.

But now, as he looked from the tent and watched Sophie get in her SUV, his gaze locked on Lilly. And the raging in his heart increased.

He knew, for some reason—over the last year—that if he was going to test the waters of maybe finding a woman to love, this was the only woman who had ever tempted him to do so.

She turned in that instant and looked toward the building as he stepped from the shadows. He waved at her to come talk to him. And when she hesitated and then started his way, he had to focus on getting the raging in his heart to stop pounding.

He needed to hear her when she spoke. He had to organize his thoughts because right now, he was hoping there could be something between them, but his focus had to be on the camp. Had to be that the two of them would create, together, the best Christmas camp for the ladies he loved. Yes, no denying it: Ida, Connie, and sweet Maggie were the ladies he called his favorite ladies, other than Nana, his Sunrise Ranch grandmother, and the ladies of Dew Drop. These three glampers reminded him strongly of the women he carried in his heart.

"I'm going to assume that you were asked the question I thought you were going to be asked. And that you agreed to help me with the ladies who are coming next week."

Her golden eyes shimmered in the light as she walked past him and into the tent. He followed her, interested beyond belief in her thoughts.

She looked around, still not answering him, and then she looked over at him and smiled. "I am. And though I can't imagine why I was asked, I'm oddly excited about it." She looked down, then straight at him; her eyes faltered. "I've never done anything like this. Never ridden a horse, never helped ladies enjoy a camping trip. Never done any glamping. I've never even had a facial or manicure, which I understand is part of this. I've always been too busy or distracted, so I'm kind of an oddball to ask. I cook—I'm a sous chef on the path to chef, but I'm not asked here for that. I'm going to be helping the ladies have a good time."

"Yes, and I'm glad you agreed." He was, but she looked very nervous. Not the confident chef he enjoyed watching cook from his chair on the inn's porch. "What's wrong?"

She sighed. "I'm going to be honest with you, Abe. I'm confident in the kitchen but I may need you to give me some direction on this. Just tell me what you need me to do because I'm not on the solid ground I'm used to. But as crazy as it sounds to me…" A large smile spread over her beautiful face.

That smile from this woman caused his stomach to fall to the ground and bounce right back up to his heart as he waited for her next words.

She let her hand flutter in the air as she continued, "I'm excited about helping out with the glamping Christmas camp. I might be able to help because I'm a good observer and learner, and Sophie said you'll be an excellent advisor."

His heart was on a rampage, thundering crazily—she thought he would be an excellent *advisor*. He wanted to laugh. Not exactly what he was hoping she'd say, but he was going to give it his all to be the best "advisor" she'd ever had.

He grinned, he couldn't help it, and was rewarded when she grinned right back at him. "This is going to be a great camp. The glamping ladies are going to love you, and I promise you, they are awesome, so I won't have to help you much, but I'm here."

She took a deep breath. "Good. That helps me have a little confidence in myself. I've heard they are wonderful, and I can't wait to meet them."

Lilly was nervous. He'd never seen her look like this other than when she'd fallen down the dune.

It was another side to her that drew him.

* * *

The next morning was a beautiful, sunshiny December day as Lilly walked into the inn. Alice, the inn's owner and also Sophie's mother-in-law—or mother, as she called her—was at the front desk when she entered the building. She was a sweet lady, and all her sons were giving her grandbabies now and that made her extremely happy.

"Good morning," Lilly said the instant she saw her.

A smile exploded across her face. "Good morning! I hear you're making my sweet daughter-in-love very happy."

Lilly loved her name for her sons' wives.

"I'm relieved that she'll get to stay home and relax before giving birth to my next grandbaby. And you're going to love it out there. You're going to be perfect for it, too. We're thrilled for you to get out there and have a good time."

"I am actually looking forward to it. I wasn't sure right away, but Sophie is a very persuasive person." She chuckled. "And I didn't even know I had an itch to have a bit of a vacation because I love my job here so much."

Lisa walked out of the kitchen in that moment and headed straight to Lilly. Then she threw her arms around Lilly, hugging her tight and rocking side to side. "You have made this not only the best vacation I've had with Zane and our sweet boy, but you made all the customers happy too." She leaned back and grinned.

Lilly's heart filled with joy, knowing she'd pleased Lisa. The woman had helped her become the chef she dreamed of being. "Thank you. That means a lot to me."

"Everyone loved your food. You are amazing, and like Sophie said she told you, though we're coming back, that doesn't mean you're leaving. We want you here as long as you'll have us. We know what a talented chef you are, and you have an amazing future anywhere you choose. Now, with that clear, I have to say how excited I am that you've chosen to help Sophie and Riley out at the camp."

"I am too," Alice agreed. "We think you'll enjoy it."

Lilly valued these two women. "It seems like a wonderful place, and I'm looking forward to meeting this group of ladies everyone seems to love." She respected these two ladies so much. Good friends, they'd both gone through hard ordeals: Alice lost her first husband and chose to buy the inn and start again. Then she'd hired Lisa, who was an amazing chef and had gone through a tough divorce. She found herself again through her talent with food and helped Alice make the Star Gazer Inn successful. The two friends showed that life always had more to offer. In that moment, standing there looking at their smiling faces, Lilly realized she wanted what they had found. She'd been through hard times and was working diligently to finally make her dream come true. Nothing would get in her way ever again.

That thought twirled around her head as she smiled

back at them. "Both of you ladies are wonderful. This inn opening gave me the opportunity of a lifetime. Like I told Abe yesterday, I've never actually had a vacation. I've never camped, and I don't know how to ride a horse. I've never actually spent time on the beach, either, so this should be interesting. And from everything I've heard, this must be a wonderful group of ladies to make a cowboy like Abe—" She paused, seeing the way both ladies looked at her.

Oh goodness, she had a feeling they had taken her words as something more than what they were.

Alice's eyes twinkled. Really twinkled, like white crystals on a giant Christmas tree, sparkling as a smile spread across her pretty face. "Abe is a wonderful guy. He's one of our number-one cowboys. And he's the best to take Riley's place while he's out with Sophie. Abe topped the list of who was best to stand in for Riley. He's a great guy and the fact that Ida, Connie, and Maggie love him dearly is proof of that. They don't hide their liking of him at all. They've come here to the inn a few times in between camps to see Sophie, and they always have dinner here with Abe. They adore him. We're glad you're going to help him, and you two will make a great team. As Lisa said, this place is always open to you, sweet girl. Our family loves you. Your cooking is amazing and yes, you could take an elite position as top chef in New York or San Francisco or any great place you chose. Right now, we're honored that you're here with us."

Her heart thundered. This was so much more than she'd expected. And yes, she had thought that maybe she would move up some in her career, but they were saying she was at the top already. They were wrong about that; however, she didn't correct them. It was sweet that they said that, but her feet weren't under her that well and there were so many elite chefs in the world…she didn't even compare. Still, she was honored that they would say such a thing.

"Thank you so much for the kind words. I'm stunned and happy. I'm supposed to go out there tomorrow, so please tell me what you need me to do before that. And help me in any way you think I need before I go out there to something I've never done before. Not cooking but instead, being a hostess for a lot of ladies who are adored obviously by everyone they meet."

Alice and Lisa both grinned so big, looking like bright lights shining in the room, causing her heart to pound with their excitement because…she was just as excited as they were.

CHAPTER FIVE

Abe watched the tent constructors finishing up putting the smaller tents on the back side of the giant tent with the concrete floor where the ladies enjoyed the dancing and evening dinners. The smaller tents were where the massage therapist would be, and one was for the manicurist and pedicurist. And then there was even one that someone would be in to do their hair. This was where all the special projects the ladies enjoyed would happen. He didn't know exactly what all that stuff was called because he didn't do them. The only thing he did was go to town and get his hair cut, put his cowboy hat back on, head back to the ranch…or here at the camp…and that was it.

Everything was looking good, so he headed back to

his trailer. When he reached his, he glanced across the firepit to the trailer where Lilly would stay. Sophie's original little trailer sat near the entrance of the camp as an inviting advertisement with its script across it that said, "Live, Laugh, Love, and Enjoy Life… It's just too dang short." He smiled, thinking about it, because it was true. Everyone who loved to camp believed it.

The trailer was what brought Riley and Sophie to meet when she pulled into a gas station with the cute trailer behind her and it first drew Riley's attention as he filled his truck's gas tank. First the trailer and its words drew his attention, and then she stepped out of her Jeep and captured all of his attention. Riley always talked about how they set eyes on each other and the quote on her trailer was now their motto. They'd had a fun, great love story and it started with the cute trailer.

Cute as it was, Abe was glad, though, that the trailer Lilly would use was a larger one with some room to move around in and not just a small bed squeezed inside and not much else. No, she had a very nice camper with a bedroom and a separate living room area, a kitchen, and a small bathroom with a shower in it. He hoped she liked it. With one last glance, he went inside his camper that also had plenty of room—not that he spent much time in it when the camps were going, but the bed was comfortable and that was a good thing.

Normally his camper was across camp, closer to the horse pens, but because he was running the show this time, Riley had moved it here to make it easier for Abe to get to everything, not just the horses. His good ranching buddies would oversee the horse riding for him, and he knew they would have a good time. Gus, the older cowboy they all respected, would be there for his first time at the camp. Also, Kurt would be here, too; he always came out to help the campers. They were similar in age, similar in attitudes, and similar in backgrounds. That was probably why they enjoyed being here so much.

He went into the bathroom, washed his hands, then raked his wet hands through his hair, smoothing it down as he stared at himself in the mirror. He took a deep breath and yeah, wished himself good luck. He wanted to make this camp great like Riley and Sophie always did, and they'd given him the opportunity because they thought he could do it. He did not want to let them down.

But also, these sweet ladies who were coming meant a lot to him and would make sure this was as memorable as could be. He smiled, feeling certain that he had a great helper. He had to make sure she got a lot out of this camp, as he did. Knowing she was going to be here any moment, he picked up his hat and placed it on his head—saw that it was slightly crooked and left it that way as he headed out of the camper.

It was time to get started.

* * *

Lilly put on her shoes, then picked up her bag. It was heavy but full of everything she needed—at least, she hoped she had everything. Yes, that had been her main conversation with Lisa and Alice yesterday at the inn: what she should pack. Alice had assured her that her girls always packed regular things a lady needed, plus blue jeans, a pair of tennis shoes that she could use instead of boots considering she didn't own any, and most likely would never need again after she rode a horse at camp.

Hopefully she got to do that along that beautiful ocean beach. She'd also packed a large-brimmed straw hat for the beach. She'd bought it when she'd first arrived here to work in the kitchen, thinking she might walk on the beach and would need it…she hadn't done that yet. The hat had simply sat on the top of her dresser, taunting her, telling her what she hadn't done. Until now she'd ignored it, but now she picked it up, and actually laughed as she placed it in her suitcase and then headed for the door.

A-glamping she would go, glamping she would… Oh yes, she would have fun, and if she made mistakes, hopefully she'd at least make someone laugh.

That was a thought that used to irritate her and fortunately, in the kitchen, she didn't make mistakes that made people laugh.

No, in the kitchen, she was a totally absorbed and capable chef, determined to make the best of herself, and mistakes didn't have a place in the kitchen with her. Thank goodness she didn't make them there. But not so in other parts of her life.

In the kitchen, she was sure-footed, and no one had seen the other part of her because she was always in the kitchen. She hoped that if she stumbled and fell again like she had done on the sandy dune in front of Abe, that at least she'd make someone smile… Abe's smile dove into her mind, and her lips curled up in response as she set her bag in the back of her Jeep.

Lilly had bought the Jeep from Sophie when she'd upgraded to a larger SUV that could carry her babies. Lilly had loved the look of the Jeep, like an adventure waiting to happen, but she'd focused—as usual—on the kitchen, and no adventure had happened. But now, as she climbed behind the steering wheel, she felt the excitement of an adventurous escapade building inside her.

Inhaling the fresh air, her gaze went to the bright sapphire sky above the quaint, affordable neighborhood she lived in. She started her Jeep, backed out, and headed down the quiet street toward the bay at the end of the neighborhood entrance. She didn't yet make enough money to put her in a house on the beach with the wonderful view, but one day she would. Still, she wasn't complaining because this blue sky was hers to see always. She turned her red Jeep onto the main road that led out of town along the coastline toward the ranch's beach. The breeze brushed her face, and her smile widened as a sense of…adventure filled her.

Adventure. Her mind reeled with the excitement building inside her even as it combined with uncertainty of doing a good job. But as she drove through the camp gate, her heart slammed against her chest when the tall, strong cowboy stepped into view—

"Oh," she gasped, as Abe lifted his hand in a wave of greeting and a wide, amazing smile spread across his handsome face. *Goodness, get control!* She moaned silently as her foot stumbled when she pressed the brake—missed and instead pressed the gas.

CHAPTER SIX

"Whoa," Abe yelled as he dove out of the way of the Jeep when Lilly had obviously pressed the gas instead of the brake. Thankfully, she yanked the steering wheel while he dove in the opposite direction, hit the ground and rolled. He rolled to his stomach and watched as she got the brake slammed down, then obviously rammed the shift into park and flung herself from the red Jeep. He rolled to his back as she reached him, terror on her face.

"I am so, so sorry," she gasped, dropping to her knees. "Are you hurt?" Her hand went to his right shoulder and the other to his right knee as she searched for damage. He lifted his chest up as he rose on his elbows and instantly her gaze dropped to his chest, then raced down his body to his legs and probably his boots from the way her hair fell between them. Then she swept her hair out of her way and locked her troubled eyes with his.

He couldn't help it; a grin took over as his heart thundered, looking into her beautiful, worried eyes. *Had she felt some of the sizzle he was experiencing?* Sizzle that had nothing to do with nearly getting run over.

Alarm took over her expression instead of awareness that she might have felt, and he sat all the way up.

"I'm okay. I really am. You've started another of my days out with an adventure." He laughed, trying to give her comfort, and he was rewarded with a sigh from her pretty lips.

She leaned back and rested her elbows on her knees, as her expression filled with beautiful relief. "I was lost in thought thinking about the week. I didn't see you until boom! You came into view, and I stomped the wrong pedal. Thankfully, you are an alert cowboy." She rubbed her forehead, her expression returning to one of horror. "What if I do something crazy like that with all the people coming?"

"You're not going to do that. You're an amazing, alert, observant chef who never makes a mistake. You'll do great. Just bring that in here with you."

She sighed deeply, her eyes mellowing. "Honestly, Abe, no one ever has seen the real me. The person you've seen two times now. I'm not the most sure-footed person anywhere but in the kitchen. My feet have minds of their own. They like to trip me up. They like to obviously stomp things and make me roll down hills. I hadn't told you that before because I was hoping maybe all my years concentrating in the restaurant would rub off on me."

"Wow, who is this woman I'm talking to? Lilly, you are a very talented person. And you bring that out in yourself in the diner. Well, not the diner—the kitchen or whatever you chefs call it. You've developed that like a master and obviously you spend all of your time in there, don't you?"

She had cupped her hands in her lap, her white jeans dusty from sliding to her knees.

He smiled, just looking at her. "Don't go telling me

you're not ready. You look ready for an adventure. Believe me, I'm a cowboy who wrangles horses, cows, goats—anything you put in front of me on the ranch. When Riley asked me to come out here and help with taking campers on horseback rides on the beach, it was a surprise." He grinned. "But I loved it. I can tell you, my first camp here was with the sweet ladies who you're going to meet tomorrow. They helped break me in, and they're going to do exactly the same thing for you. You're going to love it and be awesome." Her eyes glistened. "Thank you. I'm looking forward to it. I want to learn to do a few things I've never done before while I'm here—like maybe ride a horse on the beach. But now that you know I make mistakes, you might need to keep an eye on me and tell me when I'm doing wrong."

He stood and held his hand out to her. She looked up at him, and his heart thundered, not just in one place but all through his chest when those golden eyes met his as she slipped her hand into his. He held her hand firmly, making sure her feet were steady as she rose to a stand near him. He could have easily slipped his free arm around her, but he wasn't a dummy. He knew if he did that, he wouldn't have a chance with her. And making steps forward with this beautiful lady was at the top of his list.

The lady he knew now, more than ever, he wanted to get to know better, and he was thankful for this week. "All right then, come with me, and I'll show you where you're going to stay. You can either drive that Jeep or if you want me to drive it, I will. But I'm just going to tell you I'm confident you're not going to try to run me over again." He chuckled, trying to ease her suffering, then pointed back behind the office building to the blue trailer with the black line in it. "That's yours, so just go over there and hop inside your Jeep. I'll be waiting there for you."

She took a deep breath and gave him a cute, uncertain smile—but still a smile. "Alrighty then, here we go." She headed for her Jeep.

He watched her and then decided maybe watching wasn't what he needed to be doing, so he turned and went to stand by the blue trailer. He watched her drive cautiously toward him. He grinned, then stepped out, making sure he was exactly where she needed to park. "Come on, you're going to make it." He grinned and waved her in.

She put on her brakes as she did as he asked, then he walked to the open side of the Jeep, intending to assist her. But she was already out and lifting her duffel bag from the back of the Jeep. He slid his hand over hers, determined to carry it for her, and instantly felt the tingles from his fingertips to his toes. Her gaze flew to his; he saw sparks there that matched his.

He liked sparks. "I'll carry this for you," he offered, then took the bag as he grinned at her and headed toward her trailer.

* * *

She followed the cowboy. Yes, Abe was just a cowboy who she was here to help, nothing more.

Lilly let that make its way through her brain like it was on repeat, and she kept her eyes glued to his wide shoulders and not his slim jean-clad hips or his long legs. He was one gorgeous man, no denying that, but she wasn't here looking for romance. She was looking for nothing more than having a great experience that would enable her to become an even better chef. Communicating better with her customers was something she needed to learn.

She stepped up into the trailer. Abe had stopped just inside the trailer beside the stove and was holding her bag as he looked at her as if waiting for her to enter further and check out the trailer. The only problem was there wasn't much space, maybe two and a half feet to get past him.

"It's a great place. Where do we put my bags?" she asked.

"I'll set them on the bed, how's that?" He strode to the door at the end of the small trailer and leaned inside, setting the bag on the end of the bed that filled the small room.

Trailers were crowded. Really crowded. Her attention had been snagged by his jean-clad hips as he'd leaned into the room and now, as he turned back to her, she yanked her gaze to meet his eyes.

He grinned.

Mortified by her attraction—no, reactions—to this man, she hoped he didn't see the alarm she felt by her crazy responses to him.

"There you go. So, this is your kitchen." His words slowed as their gazes held, and he lifted his hand and motioned toward the cabinets and then waved at the door beside him. "Your shower is behind this door. And there's a coffeemaker there beside you. If there is anything you realize you need, just go to the kitchen supply area and pick out anything you want. Might want to grab some snacks… We have everything."

They were not moving, and he suddenly seemed to have trouble with his words, and she was barely thinking, so maybe it was just her.

Suddenly, the handsome cowboy became alert. "Alrighty then, I'm heading out. You get settled in and then meet me at the big tent where I was day before yesterday. I'll—I mean, *we'll* start getting everything lined up. I'll show you how to help me sign everybody in. This will be, in some ways, a learn-as-we-go process. I'll, um, get my thoughts in order—" He stopped talking abruptly, as if he realized he just said he had to get his thoughts in order.

Were his thoughts as out of order as hers? Her heart hammered against her throat; it had flown upward from the rampage of beats it was processing.

"I'll see you." And then he took three steps forward, toward her—the only way out.

She spun swiftly, so her back leaned against the counter in order to let him by. He also spun so his back was to the table and suddenly they were face-to-face as he sidestepped to move past her. There was a little bit of space between their bodies, but their gazes were locked. She was positive he heard the raging and banging going on inside her.

Then, he was past her; he reached the door and was out it in a swift two steps. It closed firmly behind him.

Thank goodness.

Instantly, she sank to the bench at the table, plopped her elbow on the table, and dropped her throbbing forehead to her palm. *What had just happened? What?*

* * *

"Gus, this is Lilly Holloway, and she'll be helping with the campers, so I wanted to introduce you. Lilly, Gus is one of our top hands out at the McIntyre Ranch. He has been there longer than me. He started working for Riley's dad before he drowned, and before I took a job here. But I thought I'd invite him out to help the ladies with their horse rides. Those ladies love to ride horses on the beach and need good fellas to help them."

Gus had swept his hat from his head and was grinning at Lilly as she smiled at the older man. Cowboy Gus was of medium height, in his late sixties, with hair the color of a white crest of an ocean wave as it rolled in, and his hair curled in like that too. He had blue eyes, the topaz color of the water. He was a cowboy but looked as though he fit in beside the ocean. Abe enjoyed the man's perky personality; now he enjoyed watching Lilly's reaction as Gus held his hand out to her.

"It's a good thing to meet you, ma'am. I'm a cowboy and like these open plains and, well, so I don't come this way much and haven't eaten at the restaurant, where I hear you're a wonderful chef." He grinned, let go of her hand, and looked at Abe. "Abe's recommendation was that I take a step forward in my life and come out and help these ladies ride horses on the beach. He said I kept to myself too much and would enjoy it—he thinks I needed a little relaxation since I don't do that much. Kind of like him—he's a worker, too. But here I am. And may I say, Lilly, you have a beautiful smile. And that makes me smile."

Lilly's beautiful smile spread wide, and her eyes glittered as she looked at Gus in shock.

Abe bit back a laugh—this good man had only been married once, lost her early to a car wreck and never remarried. But he knew how to tease ladies into smiles. And as much as Abe had been around Gus, he'd never known the man to date anyone. He'd said that he'd loved once and wouldn't ever lose love again. That suddenly struck Abe hard.

He'd never known love, might never know it but… His gaze locked on Lilly, and he focused quickly back on Gus.

This was going to be interesting to watch because he might have had an ulterior motive that he wasn't telling anyone about. He wanted to see what happened when good ole Gus met the three ladies Abe loved: Connie, Ida, and Maggie. They, along with Sophie, were the leaders of the group coming to camp. And he thought it would be fun if the sparkle he saw and was drawn to in Lilly's eyes could show up in the eyes of one of the wonderful ladies he knew were about Gus's age.

"It's really nice to meet you, Gus," Lilly said, drawing his thoughts back. "We actually have something in common. This is my first time here at camp too. So, you might have to help me find my way if you get ahead of me." Gus threw his head back and laughed, loud and vivacious. This cowboy had a good sense of humor, and it had always been fun to round up horses with him. He reminded Abe of one of the older ranch hands at the Sunrise Ranch where Abe had lived. Where Abe had found himself after a troubled time in his life. That ranch and those wonderful founders had turned it into a home for boys who needed love, direction, and an ear to talk to sometimes. That might be the reason he and Gus had gotten along so well. Gus had been an orphan also, had lost both of his parents in a car wreck when he was a little boy. But Gus had been raised by a loving couple, while Abe had found a huge, amazing family at Sunrise Ranch who he loved and would always be grateful to.

Still grinning, Gus calmed his laughter down and looked straight at Lilly. "You can count on me. I like taking care of anybody who needs help. Especially if it has to do with a horse—then I'm your man. Although this fella right here knows his business too. He's one great cowboy. Obviously, Abe loves this place. Ever since he started, he hasn't turned down an opportunity to help. Yeah, when they're not having a camp, he's out at the ranch, working cattle. But if they're having a camp and they need him, he's here. I can totally understand why Riley called on him to step in when he was going to be out having that baby with his beautiful wife. Okay, I'm talking too much, so now I'll let you talk." He laughed and pretty Lilly did too.

"You sound like you're going to be great for the place. Me, I'm not so sure. I'm a little worried about not knowing anything they might ask me. I can see that you and Abe are perfect."

Gus shot Abe a look before pinning her with his ocean eyes. "Honey, I have a feelin', and I'm sure Abe agrees, that Riley and Sophie *chose* you for a reason. From what I know, they don't pick just anybody. There's a reason you're here. I'm pretty sure you're an asset, or you wouldn't have been invited. We're going to be good for this place, *or* this place is going to be good for us. I personally don't know what I'm lacking in my life, 'cuz I'm a happy man. I get to herd cows all day, brand horses, medicate and care for animals, and that's a good life as far as I figure. I can put my feet up on my back porch and watch the sunset, or put my feet up on my front porch and watch the sunrise while I drink my coffee—coffee is the strongest thing I drink these days." He grinned and looked content but made it clear—as he always did—that he never touched alcohol.

It wasn't a judgmental comment, but one that always made Abe wonder if he'd once drank a lot and maybe had to correct it in his life. Going deep wasn't something Abe did unless someone offered it to him, and this great man never had.

"I don't drink either," Abe added, having a deeper reason, coming from a dad who'd been awful and mean when he drank. But he wasn't going there right now. "When we work out here or work cattle, we need to have our heads on straight."

Lilly's gaze took them both in and settled on him. "Y'all haven't said anything that I don't agree with on that."

He saw in her eyes that she thought there was more to his story than he'd said, and he thought maybe later he'd open up about his past. Maybe.

Right now, it was time to put on a grin and get back to making this a great day. "So, here's the deal. The guys are finishing up unloading things today, and Gus brought the horses out. He's got them already unloaded and fed, and they're ready for when the ladies get here. We like to bring them out a little bit early and let them adjust to the beach instead of the pastures. I think now's a good time to take you on a ride. Introduce you to horse riding so that when the ladies come and one of them feels uncomfortable, you can give them your experience on your first ride. Hopefully tell them how much you liked it." He was grinning when he finished but was as serious as could be. He wanted her to enjoy the thing he loved the most, the thing that had helped him find peace in a life that had once been out of his control. Horse riding was the miracle that he'd found at Sunrise Ranch. That and the wonderful family he loved.

"Horse riding…" She sighed. "Yes, I think I'd rather ride my horse the first time without a lot of people watching. You two sound like you know what you're doing, so if I can or can't, I'll have you to help me either way. So yes, let's do that."

He liked the fact that she liked what he had decided to do, and so he took a step back, waved his hand toward the direction where the horse pens were, and then he looked at Gus. "Thank you for saddling them up. We'll be back. Thank you for watching out for what else is going on for me while I take this nice lady for a ride."

"Glad to do it. Lilly, if anybody can help you ride, it's this cowboy. So, don't be afraid. He'll get you on that sweet horse I brought for you. He'll take care of you. Have a good time." And then he turned and strode away.

Lilly's gaze went from watching Gus walk away back to Abe. "I guess it's you and me?"

He liked the sound of those words and the thought of just the two of them riding out by the water together. "Yes, it is. I'm not going to brag, but you can relax 'cause Gus wasn't just saying that I am good with horses and good with people riding horses. I would never have been invited to be here if I wasn't good at helping people ride. Now, let's go check out the waves on horseback. You're going to love it too."

And so was he.

CHAPTER SEVEN

Lilly walked beside Abe to the area near the trees where the horse pens were. Excitement seeped through her. *She was going to ride a horse.*

As much as she wanted to deny it, yes, riding the horse was exciting but not what had her heart thundering in her chest. No, it was the fact that she was going riding on the beach with this handsome cowboy.

It was going to be hard to keep her focus on her life goals. It was a statement that ran through her head and was starting to drive her a little bit crazy.

As they stopped by the fence and her gaze settled on the beautiful white and tan horse, she breathed in relief. *Something else to focus on.* It was smaller than the large one beside it. "They're beautiful."

He placed his hands on the fence, and she took a step up beside him and did the same, her hands beside his as she looked at the stunning horses. Then, smiling, she turned her head and looked at Abe. Instantly, her pulse thundered at their closeness, so she focused back on the horses.

"That's Bucky, the smaller one. He's a very calm ride—despite his name. He's not huge and so I figured it would make it a little more comfortable for you to be closer to the ground in case you are worried about getting bucked off. For some, there is a fear of falling off, so he comes in handy. Things can happen, we never have guarantees, but I'll be near. And the sand would give you some padding, too. Unless we're riding out in the waves and you fall in; then you have some swimming time, too, on this ride." He grinned big.

She laughed. "Funny, really funny. I'm not a huge swimmer either."

He grabbed his hat from his head and slapped it on his leg. "Girlfriend, we have *got* to get you some experiences out here. You are an amazing chef. And I put emphasis on that word because it's true—*amazing*.

But I can tell you you're fixin' to have a really good time because riding a horse is great. Riding a horse in the sand near or in that beautiful blue water waving around your feet or the horse's feet is therapeutic. It could completely win you over. Just like it did me."

Their gazes locked, and she knew if she were ever going to pick who was going to help her learn to ride a horse, it would be Abe, this handsome cowboy. This handsome and nice man whom she'd learned had had no one for a while in his life. "I'm ready when you are. And I know you'll keep me safe…I believe that completely."

As she looked into his eyes, she knew her words were true.

In her life, men had no place anymore. The fact that she had made some "man" mistakes in her early life and had no plans to date again until she had her career as a top chef firmly in place, that tingle just standing near Abe was trouble.

It was crazy confusing; she could tell just by the way he was acting right now that he was different from any of the bums she had gotten mixed up with earlier in her life. Three men who had actually helped set her on the right direction in her career because of tossing her away…of making her feel lost, then angry until she realized she owed them for setting her head straight to focus on where she wanted to be in her life. And being attracted to this handsome cowboy was not what she needed.

Or where she would let herself go. And now, it was time to get her head on straight and to do it with a smile. "I'm looking forward to it. And I'm sure you can help anyone learn to ride in a pasture or on a beach, even me. So, thank you, and in all honesty, my friends wanted to get me out from behind the cooking counter and obviously knew *you* were the one who could help me."

His grin widened; his eyes danced, then grew serious. "I'm smiling because what you're saying is making me happy. I will keep you safe."

"I believe it. So, when you open that gate and lead the way, I'll follow you."

He opened the gate, walked into the pen, and she followed him. He closed it behind her and winked. Then he led the way across the area.

Here we go. Yes, and she was not backing out—

despite the pounding in her heart.

* * *

Abe was shocked by the excitement sparkling in Lilly's eyes. He hadn't known exactly what to expect but finding out she had never ridden a horse hadn't really surprised him. Finding out she had never been on a beach and she lived here…that had been a big shock to him. Being the one getting to be by her side while she experienced all this made his excitement about being around her increase even more.

She had never ridden. He remembered well his first time on a horse. It had been life changing for him. After his parents had basically deserted him, he had been an angry, hard kid—shut down, trying to deal with his feelings of worthlessness.

He'd been an angry guy for a while, knowing that life had dealt him a terrible deck of cards and not caring about finding his own way out.

Then he was sent to Sunrise Ranch and found out quite quickly that he was not alone. He was with a lot of young men, boys who were now men like him. Most of them had also been dealt hard portions in their life. And he had learned that even in the sons of Lydia McDermott, the woman whose dream of opening the huge ranch to boys like him were his age when they lost her, they too had to overcome inside turmoil.

Morgan, Rowdy, and Tucker had taught him that riding horses and herding cattle was the place to be when you were torn up inside. Out in the open, with the wind blowing and cows mooing, cutting up sometimes, making you work hard—that was a great place to start over. A great place to learn to deal with internal pain.

He had watched so many heartbroken guys overcome it, including those three who were now his brothers, as he called them, all those before and after him who called the ranch home. Their dad, Randolph, had then and now offered each boy who came to the Sunrise Ranch his last name if they chose to take it. His love and understanding was with them no matter what they chose, but they got to choose. Abe would have taken McDermott proudly, because his dad had been the one who caused his family trauma. But despite his mom having been so wronged, she hadn't given up on his dad, and despite her weakness and giving in to drinking and having him taken away from her, he loved her. And he'd loved her father, his granddad, so after she'd died, instead of taking McDermott, he'd taken Bradshaw, her maiden name. And was determined that when he died, he'd leave something good behind with that name.

His life had been complicated and riding horses on that enormous, awe-inspiring ranch that was fed by Texas oil, that enabled the McDermott family to house sixteen boys at a time and bring Lydia's dream to reality, gave him peace. It was the heart of the land, the learning of how important hard work and dedication was. And most of all, determination to be the best that he could be despite what came before he'd found his way. That had helped him heal and become a guy devoted to helping others but also determined to enjoy life.

And if possible, he'd find someone to share his life with. He just had never been drawn to anyone who made him think it was time, that it could happen.

He pushed the thought away—right now, it was

time to ride a horse. Despite the fact that his heart was dancing an unbelievably fast two-step as he looked into Lilly's golden eyes, he knew he couldn't rush things.

"If you will reach up there with one hand, hold onto the saddle horn and then stick that foot right there in that stirrup and lift up, then toss that other one over…I'm holding onto the reins just in case, although I have all the confidence in the world that Bucky isn't going to do anything we don't want him to do."

Her gaze locked on to the horse and then him. There wasn't any fear in her eyes but what he took as anticipation.

"I am ready, so here goes." She reached up, grabbed hold of the saddle horn, and then, using that to steady her, placed a foot into the stirrup.

He placed his hand on her lower back to make sure she knew he was there and then, in one boost, she was up and her leg was over, and she settled into the saddle.

"Well, talk about graceful…there you go. I thought you told me you could be—what were your words?—clumsy. I'll tell you there was nothing clumsy about that saddling up. You were extremely sure-footed like you are in the kitchen."

"Thank you. I knew you were standing there. Your hand on my back helped me have some confidence. So, thanks—you have good instincts."

He grinned, reached up, and held the reins out for her. She hesitated before taking them from him; their hands touched, and lightning bolts exploded inside him.

"I didn't always have that confidence," he blurted. "But my foster home, which is now my home, is in Dew Drop, Texas. They gave me confidence. And I can tell you for a guy who was angry at what life had dealt him, and just down in the bottom of the riverbed basically, I learned from watching Mr. Randolph McDermott. His wife was the one who inspired and wanted them to open the home. Miss Nana, as we all called her—his mother—was as devoted as he was to making sure they made Lydia's dreams come true. Nowadays, it's the three boys—now men about my age—who help and inspire a lot of kids. But me and those three and several more who I'll see at the family reunion soon—we were all dealt with suffering and hurt, and we all came through it okay. So, anyway, didn't mean to get sidetracked there."

"I'm so sorry that you went through what happened to you. And all those others you're talking about."

He was still standing there; she had taken the reins and had both hands on the saddle horn. His hand that had been holding the reins now rested on the side of the saddle near her thigh, just so that if something did happen he had a way to hold the horse and instantly grab that saddle. But it also gave him a closeness to her.

"I have a past, but everybody does. The key to having the life that you want is to put one foot forward, then take a step; put the other foot forward and take a step. If you make a wrong move or take a step back or, as some of my buddies and brothers have done, rolled down that hill and hit bottom again, you just get back up and start all over again."

Her eyes suddenly glistened.

That startled him. "What?"

"I have a past, too, and I have tried and am trying to keep making those steps forward instead of backward. The last thing I want to do is roll back down that hill. I've worked hard to get up here to the top of it, being the chef I want to be so that I can make the life that I want. I've done good, and I think it looks like you have too."

Her voice wavered, telling him how sincere and heartfelt her words were. "Thank you. So now that I know that little bit about you, just know that I'm here for you. You're doing great, whatever happened to you. From here, it looks like it's all gone."

"I'm not to the top of the hill yet, and I won't be until I feel like I'm the best chef I can be. That when someone sits down at my table, they feel like they're eating the most delicious and entertaining meal they've ever eaten, made with my two hands, or at least my creative mind and awesome sous chefs assisting me."

Wow, this woman had a dream, and it came first… But as he stood there looking up at her, he had to wonder whether, like him, she might ever think about adding a partner to that landscape after she reached her goals.

CHAPTER EIGHT

Lilly's heart had cinched as she told Abe her dreams. After listening to his words, all he'd been through, she knew those around him had been through just as much or more, and this amazing cowboy had empathy for them while he held strong to himself.

He swung into his saddle with swift, professional, and very masculine moves of the well-developed cowboy that he was. That he had been determined to become. And now, as apparent in his every action and word spoken, he rode beside her, encouraging her, instructing her on everything she needed to become a confident, capable rider.

They were now past the sand dunes, using a trail that enabled them and all the other riders never to ride a horse over a sand dune. Which she was grateful for and almost laughed, envisioning Bucky and her tumbling backward down the dune. She probably wouldn't have been so lucky as she'd been, though at least Abe would be near and beside her in a split second. Of course, that wouldn't happen because this small horse was smarter than she was when it came to knowing sure-footedness in the sand.

Her thoughts were locked on him and all of those guys at that place, Sunset Ranch. It wasn't Sunset Ranch; no, it was Sunrise, and she felt like all those boys who came there were like Abe and learning to watch the sun rise every morning in their new life.

As her horse stepped into the first small bit of water, feeling steady beneath her, her mind whirled with the thought of sunrise. She looked over and Abe was riding in the water on her far side, putting him between her and the water as if he were her shield. He was watching her.

"You're riding great, but you looked troubled."

"Oh." She garbled the singular word as it came out of her throat. She fought for steadfastness. "I'm good. My brain just rolled out into the waves or something.

It's all back now. This is awesome." She forced her brain from thinking about the cowboy and let the breeze rush over her as she focused on it and the beauty before her. A smile bloomed instantly and suddenly, for the first time in a very long time, she felt free.

Free? Where had that come from?

"There it is again, but this time the look is happier, not unsettled. Am I close?"

Wow. "You're observant and yes, you're close. I feel free and the feeling shocked me. Sitting here, feeling the security of this horse, knowing what he's doing walking through the water lapping around his ankles, and the sun on my face and the wind blowing in my hair…the feeling of free just infused me."

He smiled instantly—whoa, a brilliant smile she had never seen before—and her pulse reacted by skyrocketing to the sun beaming down on them.

She smiled in response, incapable of anything else—the man just sent joy through her when his eyes sparkled and he smiled a little bit—but this smile and her internal response was unbelievable.

"There, that is what I like to see. You just let loose,

didn't you?"

Let loose. Of what?

Her past?

Her fears?

She did not know, wasn't going there. But what she did know was she loved riding a horse. "I think I'm hooked. I think maybe I understand why people ride horses. I don't know if it's the same in a pasture but right here on this beautiful beach, I totally understand."

"It's similar on a ranch. It's a lot of things. It depends on what you're going through. It can be a place to let your anger out, I'm telling you. I rode and broke horses that were wild. I rode them across those pastures like I was running myself, and the horses were getting broke, so they loved feeling free.

"It was like their last hurrah before they eventually settled down and became tamed. The horses knew when to let themselves hold back and when to hold nothing back. They were great. The ranch had unending pastures that worked out to be great therapy for the horse and angry, rejected boys, the sad boys, confused boys, and sometimes desperate boys riding on their strong backs."

"Wow," she whispered, caught up in the vision he'd created.

He held her gaze. "I think it works the same for everyone. So, I'm glad we came riding. I don't yet know what's going on in that head of yours…I have to say, that *beautiful* head of yours. And I'm not going to barge in—but I'm going to assure you that I'm here, and I've been through a lot and seen a lot through the lives of my brothers. And I'm just letting you know that, like I am and was for them, I'm always here to help. Me, I'm a walking, talking survivor, and I'm proud to be who I am. I'm here to tell everyone and anyone that if I can do it, they can. I didn't let the life that had been thrown at me take me down. I could have, but God put me in a place where I could cope. And not just cope—I could learn to live as I was. Learn to love what I was doing and how I was living and everybody around me. So anyway, if you need to talk about it, you just let me know."

"You are amazing." The words came out and lifted on the soft breeze as her gaze latched onto his.

"I'll just tell you there is a spot in my life that I couldn't step over," he said, softly. "But I know, right now, that I'm ready. And I just want to tell you that when you know you're ready, you're ready. Until then, you just keep pushing your way up that hill. And I know you will. Not only will you be the best chef in the world, if that's what you want to be, when you finally finish your trip, you'll also be happy. And that's the stage that I have settled into right now. I'm happy. I felt driven to move out here. And I love it." His smile lifted as his gaze left her and went to the aqua-toned, white-tipped sea.

Hers followed, her heart pitter-pattering with every break of the gentle waves and every breath she inhaled. The tightness in her chest eased, despite the way looking at him affected her, making her blood pressure rise. His words though sent a peace over her and now, the strain and stress lessened even more, and she thought about everything Abe said. She wondered what he was talking about—that place he'd finally reached—was it like her wanting to be the best chef in the world?

Something told her it was different as, sitting there in the saddle of her horse beside him in his saddle, they watched the beauty before them. She took a deep breath;

her smile filled her face completely and her heart calmed with the rolling of the waves as peace seeped through her.

Peace. She hadn't felt this, ever. But in that moment, she felt it strongly while surrounded by this beautiful water, the sand, the shimmering blue sky, and the sunlight…and this cowboy by her side.

* * *

Abe wasn't sure what had happened on that horse ride, but one thing he knew was he was heading in the right direction.

There was no denying that he was or could be falling in love with the chef who had ridden out here beside him. He'd pushed that thought to the back of his heart and head as they finished the ride, not wanting to do anything to mess up whatever it was that she was going through.

By just the look in her eyes, she had discovered that a horse ride could be more than just getting on a horse's back and walking through the pasture or in the sand.

Like him…he had found peace, comfort, and closure in it, and something told him that she had found something out there today.

When they got back to the arena, she had let him help her off the horse. He had told her how to bring her leg over and step down. Unable to stop himself, he'd wrapped his hands, one on each side of her waist, to made sure she settled onto the ground comfortably, safely. He told himself it was to make sure a misstep didn't mess up her experience. But when her feet touched the ground, he had quickly let go of her and stepped back. His blood was rushing through him like he'd never felt before and not wanting anything he did to take that smile from her face, he released her.

He felt that she had let go of something out there, and he didn't want to interfere with that. But he couldn't help but wonder what had gone on in her life that she needed to let go of. She'd softly thanked him for the wonderful ride, then gone to her trailer, and he'd stayed where he was, giving her—and himself, too—space.

Later, they'd met, and he'd taken her on the tour of each building and what they were used for and then they'd gone to the office. He'd shown her how to check everyone in when they started arriving the next day and told her not only would the people be arriving but the workers too: the college students who would be working the breakfast and lunch stand, and the other cowboys who were going to help because Riley wouldn't be there.

Tomorrow would be a busy day, and he was looking forward to seeing his three favorites: Maggie, Ida, and Connie. And he knew—yup, he knew—that those three smart ladies were probably going to pick up on what was going on in his head…his heart. He just had to figure out what to do about that. So he focused on getting the camp ready. Not on figuring out his heart.

He also had to figure out supper.

He hadn't asked her to cook anything and wasn't even sure whether she had realized that they weren't having supper yet, so he was going to just grill steaks on the barbeque pit. He was a little bit nervous; after all, she was a great chef, and he was just a cowboy who loved a steak on a pit. He hoped just having a night off—actually, a week off—would be good for her.

When they finished lining up everything needed for tomorrow and were heading back toward their campers, he looked at her. "I've kept my mouth shut until now, because I was afraid you'd run for the hills, but now there's no hiding. I'm cooking dinner tonight."

She halted and grinned. "You're cooking?" Her voice had an uplift in it and made him happy.

"Yes, ma'am, at your service. Now, don't get me wrong—you're the chef and I'm just the guy who will put a couple of steaks on the pit out here and see if you like it. I've got some new potatoes that I'll be cooking on the stove in my camper. I learned it from Miss Nana back at Sunrise Ranch. That sweet lady knew how to cook. She'd take those pink potatoes and all of us boys would help chop them up in the kitchen. Then she'd put them in the water to boil and soften them up, then trade the water for milk. And after they got just right, she'd add secret ingredients to make them delicious."

"Sounds yummy," Lilly cooed, her eyes twinkling in the dimming light.

Food—think about food. "It's one of my favorites, and I think you'll like them." He grinned and hoped he cooked them like Nana had taught him.

"I can't wait." They started walking again, the trailers in view. "I'll tell you, after today, you've prepared me for this great camp, and I have to say I'll enjoy just sitting here by a fire." She stopped walking beside one of the wooden chairs around the firepit and across from the barbeque pit. "But if you'd like me to help, I will. And I promise I won't step over any lines that you may put up."

He laughed—whooped, actually. "You can step over anything you want to, but I would really like you to relax because our week starts tomorrow. I'll try hard to feed you good so you can relax by the fire and watch the twilight of the evening. And then, hopefully you'll sleep good, because I can't guarantee how much you'll get after everyone arrives. They come from all over the state, so tomorrow will be an all-day event and busy in all manner of ways."

"Then, I'll sit down and enjoy myself. I'm sure you're going to do a great job, and I'll enjoy watching you work your magic."

CHAPTER NINE

The morning after an amazing steak cooked by Abe, Lilly was up and soon very busy, and though she and Abe had enjoyed their meal very much, she'd had to head to bed early. Not because she really needed to but because she knew that was the safest place for her to be when she sat there and found herself enjoying his company beneath the beautiful moonlight with a fire burning and a gentle breeze. Of course, once she was snuggled into her bed, comfortable and alone with only her thoughts, where did they go? Right back beneath the moonlight with Abe. Yes, he was attractive, and she liked him, but that was as far as she would let it go. Her real excitement was for the camp. And today, she would know she was right. These ladies were excited to be here and clearly loved Abe. The cowboy got a hug from every woman as they came through the gates.

He had not been joking when he'd said it was going to be busy.

And he wasn't wrong. She'd been startled by the wave of people as they began to show up. Some even before opening time. She and Abe had met at the office before eight a.m. and there were already four trucks pulling charming campers, waiting in line. Fun trailers, similar to the cute one that sat at the front gate.

One was blue with big white stars painted all over it and the words, "Twinkle, twinkle, let's go glamping," and another said, "I'm a glamper, not a camper!" And the third one said, "It's not a one-horse open sleigh, but glamping all the way!" And more came, just as fun, throughout the day.

She chuckled as she read each of them—obviously all these ladies had a sense of humor, and she loved it so far.

They all talked happily as they waited for her and Abe to check them in and then to drive to their spot. Kurt, the cowboy over the horse riding, along with Gus, were helping them find their parking spaces and setting up where needed.

All the ladies were excited to be here, and she couldn't blame them. Then a small yellow pickup truck pulled in and behind the wheel sat a very happy-looking lady. She parked her truck; Abe opened the door, and she hopped out and engulfed him in a hug. Lilly watched, smiling; it was so filled with excitement. He was beaming, and it was obvious this was someone else very special to him.

And then he turned toward her, his arm around the woman's shoulders. "Lilly, I'd like you to meet Maggie from San Angelo, Texas—she loves it so much she calls it *Saint* Angelo. Maggie, I'd like you to meet Lilly. She'll be helping me host you great ladies this week."

Smiling, Maggie's pale-green eyes dug into Lilly as she took hold of her hand and squeezed it, then patted the top with her free hand. "Funny man, I do love where I live but my goodness meeting you makes me love this place more and more. We're excited that our Sophie is having a baby and that you're filling in for her, along with our sweet Abe."

Maggie, still holding Lilly's hand, looked from her to Abe, as if... *Surely this woman wasn't already trying to match her up with handsome cowboy Abe.*

And why had she called him *handsome cowboy Abe*?

Finally, Maggie let go of Lilly's hand and placed her fist on her hips, grinning widely. "You don't have a voice?"

Only then did she realize she had not said anything. "It's really nice to meet you, Maggie. I've heard that you and your two friends are wonderful and are going to be a huge help while Sophie and Riley are home getting ready for their new baby."

"We love it here. And sweet Sophie and Riley have the best man in place to fill their spot with this great guy." She grinned at Abe and again, Lilly saw a connection between the two. "Looking forward to helping with the camp, too, so whatever you need, me and my friends are here to help."

"Thank you. I'm looking forward to getting to know all of you. And Abe assures me that you and your friends are the best."

"Isn't that sweet of him." Maggie elbowed a grinning Abe. "We're going to have a fantastic time. And we're going to go visit Sophie and maybe watch that little fella kick his mommy in the belly." She laughed. "That doesn't sound good but it's always fun to watch."

Lilly chuckled, not that she had ever felt the kick of a baby in her belly and knew it would be a long time before she would, if she ever did…but this was cute and tempting… She'd been a woman who'd let the thought of marriage and family lead her the wrong way three times…*three times.*

And each one had been a disaster. She'd given up and finally gone nonstop to make her original dream of becoming a chef her one and only focus.

Yesterday, for that brief moment, you faltered…

"Lilly's going to be great and enjoy herself at the same time, I'm hoping," Abe's words drew her back from thoughts of yesterday.

She met his gaze, and it told her he had realized she'd gotten lost in thought about something. He was probably getting used to the fact that she did that sometimes.

She wasn't; she hadn't had this problem in a long time. "I hope so," she said.

His lip hitched upward. "She's going to do wonderful, and you ladies are going to help her."

"We are excited to help you, Lilly. Okay, y'all sign me in and get me out of the way of that long line I see coming down the road. Like me, I know they're ready to have a great time."

With that, she signed in and then headed to her truck. But Lilly saw her shoot a wink at Abe before she walked away.

"You are *very* popular. All the ladies who come have said hello and have been glad to see you. I know that's from your horse riding, but like you had mentioned, there was something more there between you and Maggie."

"Yeah, there is. More Maggie than the other two sweet ladies you'll meet. They are all three awesome but somehow or another, me and Maggie really connected. And she likes you too."

She chuckled. "Oh, you think so? Well, I'm just

going to say it—I don't know why I'm saying it, but I think she was sizing me up."

He hitched a brow. "Sizing you up?"

Why did I say that? "Well, I guess if you don't know what that meant, then I'll just let it slide under the rug and we'll forget about it."

His grin widened, grew huge, as his eyes sparkled teasingly. "I guess I'll just have to figure that out on my own. But I think I know what you meant."

Did she hope he did or didn't?

Didn't was her hope, because she had no business saying it in the first place. She wasn't looking for someone to be fixing her up with a guy she wasn't looking for. Yes, he was amazing, handsome, sweet, nice, kind—*everything that you could possibly describe a good man as*—but she wasn't looking.

No! She wasn't. And she suddenly was hoping very hard that Maggie wasn't about to get on the wrong road.

* * *

Later that afternoon, after everyone was checked in and

gathered under the big tent at their meet-and-greet opening night with refreshments and appetizers, Lilly could see how much the group enjoyed each other. Hugs and immediate conversations were taking place all over the large tent. The food was catered by a wonderful restaurant from a nearby town, and Lilly was very impressed. The ladies had chosen a great place; they knew good food, that was apparent.

Yes, her not cooking was kind of different, but she was doing fine, enjoying meeting the ladies who had all, so far, greeted her with smiles and hugs, and she wanted them to have something good to eat.

"*Sooo*, we hear that you are a chef," Connie said, a very nice lady from Crocket, Texas, and one of the three ladies who would be helping Lilly in any way she needed it.

"That interests us *very* much," Ida added. She was in her fifties, with soft gray and brown interlaced chin-length hair, and the third of the three ladies. She was from Midlothian, Texas, outside of Dallas.

All three ladies were nice and looking at her now with interest. "Yes, I'm a sous chef right now. That means I'm working my way up the chef ladder. My two bosses are great people and top chefs, Lisa and Zane Tyson. Just recently, I watched over the Star Gazer Inn restaurant while they took time off being parents. They were out with their new baby. It was a wonderful experience. I absolutely love being a chef." It was so true.

She realized she'd called herself a chef. She had to get used to being back in the sous chef category. It didn't bother her. She loved it here on Star Gazer Island and becoming a full-time chef and executive chef would mean moving. She wasn't yet ready to say goodbye to Star Gazer Island, nor was she to the level she believed she needed to be to fulfill her dream of being top in her field and getting a dream job—one that would eventually enable her to have the well-known reputation, then open her own place and draw customers in.

"Well," Maggie said, a huge smile on her face. "We have a wonderful idea, and we hope you will agree to go along with it."

"Yes, we hope," Connie added quickly.

All the ladies were grinning and their eyes twinkling.

"Um, sure. What are y'all thinking?"

Connie hitched her brows. "What if you taught us a couple of cooking classes while we're here? Two days would be awesome, because we're all infatuated with food. Not that we'll ever be as good as you, because we've heard that you are *amazing*. But we know it would be fun to have some lessons and it's something we've never done on our camping trips before."

They wanted her to teach them to cook something special!

The idea sent her nerves racing. "I'm so flattered," she managed as the thought settled over her. *Cooking class...* "Honestly, I love the idea. I would really enjoy doing that, if y'all are serious."

"We're very serious," Ida said first, and the others agreed.

Connie placed her hand on Lilly's arm. "Believe me, when Sophie told us she hoped to get you to fill in for her, we got excited. We've eaten a few times at the inn when the three of us came for a visit and we know you're talented. Everyone raves about your cooking and from what we're hearing, you will be moving on soon to take a top spot or open a place of your own."

The words stunned her. *Everyone was expecting her to move on?* She planned to, but people voicing her thoughts was hitting home. "One day," she said. "But I love where I am right now."

"Of course you do—it's wonderful," Ida agreed. "We're just glad you haven't done it yet because this is going to be a great camp with your added extra."

"*Soo,*" Maggie sung, "we sent out a little note asking if anyone would be interested in a cooking class from you, and everyone has responded with excitement. So, when will we start?"

Delight erupted as she glanced around at all the smiling, enthusiastic-looking faces of the ladies who had gathered around. "Let me talk to Abe and make sure that it's okay, since this is something new. He needs to tell me if it's a go and if so, when there's a good time to pursue it and to get the ingredients and utensils we'll need. How does that sound?"

"It sounds perfect, but we can already tell you," Ida

grinned, "he will say it is just fine 'cause I can tell you, dear, that good-looking cowboy already likes anything you do. And he might even come to a cooking class if you invite him."

Her thundering heart halted as if it had had the brakes slammed on, and she probably would have stumbled if she had been walking. "No, uh, this would be just for the women, right?"

All the ladies were now grinning, making it obvious that they had seen her expression. It had probably been one of sheer fear.

Fear—yes, fear that Abe would be included. And though they didn't know—at least she didn't think they could know, considering they hadn't even been here a whole day yet—*she* had figured out that every moment spent with him was dangerous.

Clearly these ladies knew he was a wonderful guy and single. *Were they hoping she might like him? Were they hoping she and Abe could—* She halted the thought. It was a compliment, actually, she realized, the fact that these smart, nice ladies thought she might be a good match or at least good enough to date Abe. She bit back a gasp. *Surely not—they just met her.*

"Don't worry, honey." Connie patted her shoulder. "You go ask him, and we'll be here enjoying this wonderful food. But, believe me, we are looking forward to maybe tomorrow afternoon for cooking class—ladies, what do y'all think of making it a dessert class?"

Everyone cheered in agreement, and all looked at her with smiling excitement. Lilly's heart thundered like it had started to do on a consistent basis.

She smiled at the ladies. "Y'all are amazing. I'll go find Abe, and I'll come back and let you know."

Ida winked at her. "I saw him earlier checking out the firepits near the beach. If you go that direction, you'll find him."

She felt all eyes on her as she walked toward the exit. The music playing in the background was a well-known older song—"Oh, What A Night"—and she couldn't agree more.

Everyone was supposed to be eating and enjoying themselves, and instead they were watching her.

CHAPTER TEN

Abe listened to the music drifting from the main tent and hoped Lilly was having a good night as he checked each of the firepits that were set up around the area for groups to gather. He was double-checking that they were in good working condition. Ready for the ladies who enjoyed spending time out beneath the moonlight and stars.

He started to go into the party but decided to let the ladies enjoy getting to know Lilly without him being there. He had talked with many of them and like Connie, Ida, and Maggie, he could tell that they were excited about Lilly being here. He had just finished lighting the firepit on the far side of the area and the one closest to the water when he was startled to see Lilly walking across the sand in the moonlight.

His insides churned as he watched her move gracefully across the sand. She had flat sandals on, white jeans that were folded up at the ankles, and a soft-pink short-sleeved top. Frozen in place, he watched as she came directly toward him. She'd almost made it when he realized she wasn't smiling or grinning; she had a troubled look on her moonlit face.

He stepped forward. "Is something wrong?"

She halted in front of him. "Yes, I think so. The ladies are wonderful, just like you said. They are so very welcoming, and I'm having a great time meeting them all. I can tell you, they are all crazy about you."

"I feel the same for them. So, what's wrong?"

She looked away, then back. "They had a question for me, and I have to ask you to see if what they're wanting is okay to do."

He cocked his head to the side. "What would they be asking you that you have to ask me?"

"They want me to teach a couple of cooking classes this week."

"Really." He grinned.

"They said they had sent out an email once they learned I was going to be here, asking everybody if it was something they would be interested in and *all* of them are wanting it."

He grinned wider. "Those are some smart ladies right there. You're one of the best chefs around, so they picked well. But the question is, do you want to do this? This is supposed to be kind of your week off from being a chef. I think it's a great idea, but it's completely up to you." He pulled his hat off and raked his hands through his hair, his mind troubled, not knowing how she felt and not wanting to make the wrong suggestion.

Her gaze followed his hand as he raked his fingers through his hair and his pulse quickened as her gaze met his.

Suddenly, in that moment, he envisioned *her* running her pretty fingers through his hair.

Whoa, whoa, whoa.

The moonlight sparkled on her hair and wasn't helping him as he tried to straighten up his thoughts. But in that moment, standing there, looking at that beautiful woman, the woman he thought was the most beautiful woman in the world, he wanted to reach out embrace her.

Wanted to sneak a moonlight kiss—

He was in trouble.

* * *

The moon shining over them, the soft sound of the water to the right of her, and the sweet, soulful music drifting all this way from the tent was not helping Lilly as the amazing cowboy met her gaze. Caught her watching his fingers run through his hair. Caught her wishing it were her fingers in those gentle waves. Their gazes locked; her insides trembled, and she had to fight off the sudden urge to step toward him.

This was a moonlit night she hadn't ever envisioned. She couldn't move, couldn't look away, couldn't help herself. Yes, she was in trouble.

All of her thoughts from years ago about the terribleness of ever getting drawn to someone again were distant, as if the incoming flow had pulled them out and tossed them to sea. Those were thoughts and lessons learned she thought would never bother her again. And, until this moment, never had.

Only this pull, this need to throw herself into this wonderful man's arms was stronger than all of the pulls she'd ever felt thrown together—none of those early feelings even compared to the magnetic draw she felt in this moment.

He stepped toward her, his gaze floating across her face and resting on her lips, then back up to hers. Her heart pounded loudly in her ears. Her breath was short as he lifted his hand and gently tucked a piece of hair, tickling the edge of her face, behind her ear. His fingers…their touch lingered there and then slid behind her neck, tender in their feel as he gently pressed against her neck. As if testing to see whether she would take that final step between them. And, to her amazement, she did.

One second, she'd been standing apart from him; the next, she was standing with just a breath of air between them. His free hand slid to her lower back and gently pressed. She couldn't breathe as her sane voice yelled, *Step back!* But her brain, here and now, in this moment wanted nothing but to kiss this cowboy.

A-glamping we will go, a-glamping we will go… The words sang through her as he leaned his head toward her, and all she wanted was to feel this handsome cowboy's lips on hers.

* * *

Abe lowered his lips to Lilly's. Her beautiful eyes had pulled him in and now his pulse pounded as their lips met. He felt her stiffen and then instantly relax into the kiss. He wasn't sure where this was going. He wasn't sure if he was acting right. All he knew was that he was kissing the woman who had begun to steal his heart from the first moment he saw her.

She'd been walking out of the Star Gazer Inn kitchen, carrying a large piece of cake with a candle burning to a couple celebrating their fifty-year wedding anniversary. She'd smiled beautifully as she'd surprised them and set the cake before them. And he'd never seen a more compelling smile, or eyes that looked so sweet as in that moment.

And he'd been drawn to steady eating there ever since.

But until now, he had never realized just how deep his pull toward her could be. He moved his hands, one into her hair and the other pulling her closer as he deepened his kiss. Her arms were around him, and the sanity came back—*how would she look at this?* He paused, forced his lips from hers and looked into her moonlit eyes. And as he did, saw exactly what he feared: a shift from lost in the moment to shock.

"I think I might have overstepped," he said, gently.

"I can't let you blame yourself," she managed, her voice gruff. "But I need you to let me go."

At her words, he pulled his hands away and she stepped back. He had just gone crazy, but his heart pounded. He had messed up and was worried. But despite all that, she'd felt perfect in his arms.

"So now that we have stepped across any boundaries that we might have seen or not seen, *you* call the shots. Tell me what you want me to do."

* * *

"We…" she started. "Can we just forget that happened? Because I'll just tell you, it's not going anywhere. I'm a loner. I messed up three different times because of my bad choices, so I can't do this."

"Men?"

He had automatically figured out what she had meant. *Was she that see-through?*

She nodded. "Yes, I was younger and made three different wrong choices. I-I thought twice I was in love, but the first one dropped me and walked away. And then I fell for the second one, and he also did the same. They just dropped me and walked away, and then what did I do—I thought I was on the way to loving another man. I was crazy. And all that time, I had put my dream of becoming a chef on pause. After that third really stupid mistake I made, I declared, never again."

"Never loving someone?"

"Yes, never putting my true dream on hold again because of my crazy heart. Maybe one day after I become the chef that I'm determined to become. I can't, I won't let myself fall apart again. Please believe me…that's not me saying you're a bad person. I think you're amazing. I just don't date or take a chance on faltering on my goal. I'm almost there and I can't—"

"Stop. I'm not those guys. I would never make you think I was somebody and then not be that person. I'm really attracted to you. I have been for a very long time. Why do you think I come to the inn and sit over there at that table in the corner—no, I'm not a stalker. I just enjoy seeing you, and your food is amazing. I'm hooked but I don't stare at you."

She knew he didn't. But her mind was whirling, and she was speechless.

"Lilly, you interest me. You are dedicated to what you do and it's obvious you thoroughly enjoy it. Everybody enjoys working with you, that's very clear. And the ladies here at this camp are going to enjoy you teaching them. That's why you were the perfect choice to step in for Sophie. I'm really glad they chose you. Don't let my kissing you mess up this whole week. I want you to really enjoy it. If you need to just forget that happened, I'll do everything I can to pretend it didn't happen. But I'm going to be blunt—I'm not usually attracted to anyone. My life was hard and rough until I made it to the Sunrise Ranch and let all my anger go and let my heart find peace and happiness finally. I don't risk that."

His words drilled into her, and his eyes got so full of sincerity as he spoke. Her heart raced; she fought off wanting to step close to give him a hug and assure him that she wasn't thinking bad of him. But doing that would not be the right thing, especially after what she had just told him.

The man infatuated her.

Infatuated her like no one else had ever done. She couldn't help it—then it hit her. "You sit in that chair, that table with the worst view at the inn on purpose? Just so you can see me?" This was crazy; she shouldn't have said that. She should have just let it drop. *But was he infatuated with her?*

He took a breath. "I'm sorry, but you are the best view. And I'm not just staring at you because you're beautiful. I enjoy watching you do something you truly love. That's what I do—I'm here, I'm ranching because I love it. It's my destiny. I went through a really hard young life, but ranching got me through it. And I enjoy it. I'm going to step across a line, again, but it's obvious those other three guys weren't right, or smart. I believe strongly you're destined to be an amazing chef, but you're an even more amazing person."

His words trailed over her like warm honey as they stared at each other in the moonlight, with the sound of soft waves beating out a gentle rhythm of…the meeting of the hearts.

She yanked her thoughts to reality. "I'm flattered and so glad you found where you belonged. Now, we're going to step away from that kiss." Her voice shook when she said the words, and she girded up her insides hard. "And we're going to give these glamping ladies the best time they've ever had. So, you set me up what time you think is a good time tomorrow, and I'll let those wonderful ladies enjoy creating a mouthwatering dessert."

His eyes shadowed but then he smiled, and his eyes shined with light. "Very well then. You tell me what you need, and we'll set it up after lunch, giving us time to get the groceries delivered. And when you get the desserts ready, how about we serve them with dinner?"

She smiled. "I think that's a perfect plan." She turned and walked away, made herself not run. She had to get her head on straight and her heart… She just needed to think about tomorrow and the food she was going to help a load of ladies prepare.

She'd think about the joy she'd help bring to their hearts…not hers.

CHAPTER ELEVEN

He was in trouble. He watched as Lilly walked away. His head was spinning. The music grew louder as obviously the ladies had started their dancing. They always had a good time as every one of them got out on the dance floor together. They loved singing along with tunes from all decades. They danced together as if they were celebrating being alive and well, and it was fun to watch.

He knew that it was a good time for Lilly to head back inside. Hopefully she'd be pulled out onto the dance floor and be distracted from what had just happened between them.

Him, he needed time alone. So, he headed toward the water. Walking through the dunes, he reached the moonlit water. There he yanked his hat off and slapped it hard against his leg as he ran his free hand through his hair. It was a habit he'd had all his life, dealing with emotions that were hard to hold inside. But usually, it had been from anger. Anger at his dad and then his mother for not loving him enough to hang on for him but instead drank herself away because she missed the man who had dumped them both.

He'd been left behind, angry and torn up inside. But thankfully he'd been sent finally to the newly opened Sunrise Ranch. The place he found life and love again. But he'd never felt the draw to a person like he felt when he just thought of Lilly.

Now, he fought to get a grip on the hard emotions thundering through him. Not until tonight had he ever let himself think there could be a happy family for him to create. Not until he'd taken her into his arms and kissed her.

And she'd kissed him back.

Nothing in his life had ever felt so right.

His mind whirled as he paced through the sand to the edge of the water, hat still in his hand. He slapped his leg with it, and he stared out across the water. He just stood there, holding his breath and trying to hope that the lack of oxygen would get his brain going right again.

He held his breath so long he could hear his heart thundering; finally, he breathed but his brain wasn't on straight even then. Because in that glimmering moonlight, he still saw Lilly's golden eyes and knew he had to find a way to change her mind.

* * *

Her heart was in a hissy fit as Lilly reached the tent. The dancing had started, and she needed the ladies to distract her. She entered the tent, pushing away thoughts of how it felt to be in his arms. *And that kiss…*

And the way he had talked to her afterward. The gentle way he had told her about his past and supported her.

That had never happened.

Never. The other men had laughed at her wanting to be a chef. All three of them had demanded her time, her focus, and she had given it to them. And she had let her dream slide away.

And now, as she saw Connie waving and grinning at her, she walked forward. But on her mind was the fact that Abe had stepped back and agreed to not get in her way. But there was a tug inside her heart that wished he hadn't.

The ladies swarmed around her, grabbed her hands, and swept her onto the dance floor. Her mind was still whirling on the fact that Abe had backed off and encouraged her, and that was what had her whole attention.

"Lilly." Connie giggled as she moved to the rhythm of the music. It was a soft swing song, and everybody was dancing happily to the music, smiling and singing along with the song.

They were having a blast. Each of them had lost their dancing partner; as far as she knew, they'd had their love and lost them but that didn't take their joy away.

"Come on, girlfriend. You've got something on your mind right now. Let it go…just let it go and enjoy this moment. Dance and let your spirit rise. That's what it's for—helps you relax, helps a lot of us get our minds back on straight. Helps us remember the ones we loved to dance with, and we know that they're cheering us on from up above. So, we come, and we dance. So come on…we're going to have a good time."

She couldn't help herself; she wanted to hug that sweet lady because her heart swelled and the music bloomed and everybody around her was dancing and having a good time. In that moment, she shoved all of her other thoughts aside and did exactly what these women had all learned to do—enjoy themselves. And so she did, hoping to let her brain get straight as she relaxed with the music and the laughter of all those surrounding her. Maybe tomorrow things would be better.

Maybe tomorrow her thoughts wouldn't be stuck on Abe standing in the moonlight.

* * *

The first morning of camp was always busy. The ladies

had settled in; they had had their welcome party and they had stayed up late. Some of the ladies got up early but a lot of them slept in. Abe—he had a busy day, so he was up early. He had not come to his trailer until late, making sure everybody was in for the night. And also making sure he didn't run into Lilly before she turned in for the night.

He had already upset her enough, and he had glimpsed from a back area of the tent that she was on the dance floor and all the ladies were giving her a good time. She danced well; she didn't get carried away with it—looked almost hesitant, actually. Then he had felt bad watching her and turned away. He walked back to keep an eye on the ones gathered outside around the firepits. That was his job, he reminded himself, while he was here: safety, fun, and happiness for everybody, and making sure that everybody left with a want to come back next time.

Riley was depending on him. Abe whacked himself in the head a few times as he lay in bed, his mind stuck on Lilly. He couldn't take his focus off what his job was. But he also could use that as an excuse not to let his mind set on her. If all went well, that was his way of not messing things up. She wanted to be a chef and that didn't mean she wasn't already one, but he let it thunder in his head that her being a chef might mean moving to New York or California. Or some other big place where chefs made names for themselves. Not staying here in this beautiful small town of Star Gazer Island.

Until Lilly came along, he had never even thought about a chef. Food was food—good, bad, or terrible. But now he understood being a good chef meant great things and large horizons. He knew that remaining as a sous chef—a second-in-command—was not her dream.

So he hadn't slept well, but he was up and at 'em early. People were smiling. The kids had opened the breakfast room—well, not the breakfast room but breakfast diner. Some women were taking a long walk on the beach, wearing their shoes and fancy jogging outfits. Some of them were brightly colored; you could see them a mile away, but they were grinning. As he was turning to head back up the sand dune after checking on them, he heard his name called. He turned and sure enough, the women in the brightly colored outfits were

Ida, Connie, and Maggie, and they were headed toward him.

"Good morning, ladies. I see staying up late didn't keep you gals from getting out and enjoying this beautiful ocean on an early morning walk."

Ida put her hands on her hips. "You know we love it here, and our gal Sophie isn't here to lead us in our morning workouts since she's having a baby. But that's more important than us, and we totally understand. So, we're out and about."

He grinned as Connie took over. "Yes, we are talking about last night. We had so much fun, and that sweet Lilly is amazing. We had to practically pull her out on the dance floor, but she had a good time, though. When she first came in after talking to you about the cooking class, she looked a little disturbed. You have any idea why?"

She hitched an eyebrow, and his stomach turned.

Maggie cocked her head to the side. "We kind of wore her out dancing, we think, and she went to bed looking happier than she did when she first came back from seeing you. So, we're still interested in what happened."

He knew this had been coming. "Ladies, I love y'all, and Lilly and I talked, but it's her decision on whether to share it." The minute he said those words, everybody's eyebrows hitched up, and they all took a step closer to him.

Oh boy.

"Come on now, is there something going on between you two?" Connie asked.

"Ladies, I'm calling to get all the food in for the class today. She made me a list, and it's supposed to be delivered soon. I'm not sure what it is y'all are going to be making, but I know y'all will have fun. And y'all are going to do it after lunch. Can't wait to try all of y'alls desserts at this evening's dinner."

Maggie clucked her tongue, making a loud clacking noise. "You think we're going to accept that? We're glad about the class, but is there something going on between you two?"

"Ladies, my private life is my life." He hated saying that, but they never dug deep like this, and this was also Lilly's business.

"Excuse me, but all that tells us is that we might *need* to be digging in here just to take care of our sweet Lilly."

He looked all three of them directly in the eyes, making sure they knew he was not playing. "Ladies, you know me. I am not going to do something that will make y'all mad. So just back up and hold tight. What happened last night is between me and Lilly, and she would want me to say that. Lilly…" *Man, he had to say this.* "Okay, look, Lilly has had a hard time making her dream come true of becoming a chef. And a guy stepping in who might interest her is not part of her plan. So, you three, just like me, are going to have to get that in your heads. She has her plan, and nothing is going to get in the way of that. I'm not in the dreams of her future." He'd said more than he planned, and all of their mouths dropped open and their eyes glued to him.

"You kissed her." Connie's expression was vibrantly excited as her words slammed him in the heart.

"You *did*," Ida drawled out happily.

Maggie chuckled, and then gave a little squeal and threw her arms around him. She practically picked him up from the ground before putting him back down.

In shock, breathing hard from almost being squeezed to death, he then stumbled as his feet hit the ground after she let go of him.

"Ladies, whoa. I shouldn't have told y'all anything. I have a feeling that I'm in big trouble. Please, just listen to what I said, and don't tell her this. It might run her off."

"So, we're right. You did kiss her." Connie cocked her head to the side, her grin widening. "And from what I can tell and the look on your face, you don't want her to run off. And that makes us happy."

Great balls of fire—he was in trouble.

CHAPTER TWELVE

It had been a busy morning, from helping make sure everybody was getting breakfast like they wanted, to seeing the ladies heading out for morning walks…watching out the trailer window to make sure that Abe was already out and moved along before she exited her trailer just so that running into him this morning wasn't the first thing that happened. Thankfully, she had made it to the outdoor eating area without seeing him.

What they were all eating looked good. The young college students working inside the little hut were doing a good job: it was just regular sausage-bacon tortillas, sausage-bacon biscuits, and pancakes. There was orange juice, cranberry juice, maybe some grape juice, and water, and of course there was coffee and some milk. Everybody had something on their table, and they were busy talking.

And as she came around, they were talking about her cooking class today. She had had no idea a cooking class would bring such huge smiles and questions to everybody. She had decided to have ingredients for making a Black Forest cake.

It was a dream cake and was one of her favorites. It would take a few hands that could help do everything, and she figured everybody liked chocolate, meringue, buttercream icing, and cherries on top. Oh yeah, they were going to love this. She was just telling the ladies at the table—Suzy, Lucy, and Mira—what she had decided they were all going to fix, and they were excited. They were chattering away as she looked up and her breath caught. It was a wonder she didn't just pass out right there at their feet as Abe walked from between the sand dunes. The amazing cowboy strode from where he had first helped pick her up from the sand and was headed their way.

For a moment, it was as if he were walking on

drums as her heartbeat thundered with each step he took. And his face…well, his face took her breath away as his eyes found her and didn't let go.

"*Oh,* there's our handsome cowboy coming our way," Mira said, grinning up at her as her gaze—thank goodness—dropped from his and found the woman who was now tugging on the edge of her shirt. "He is a good-looking fella, isn't he? We heard rumors that there might be something going on between you two. Is it true?"

As if she had been hit with a sledgehammer, her brains came back. "No. There's nothing going on between us. We just work together."

"Are you serious?" Lucy asked, her voice saying that she didn't completely believe what she was saying.

"Well, if you aren't interested in him," Suzy, the other one said, "then what's wrong with you?"

She knew what was wrong with her. Boy, did she know. "Ladies, I'm just here to help with camp. I'm not here to be falling for some cowboy."

"Really?" Abe's deep voice said as his boots came into view where her gaze had fallen to the ground.

She forced the hysteria going on inside her down as she raised her gaze from his boots to his long, lean legs, to his waist, his chest, and then that good-looking face with those eyes staring at her with a twinkle in them.

He thought this was funny. He knew that probably every woman at this camp was thinking that they were going to be a matchup. It slammed into her suddenly that this group of ladies had watched Sophie and Riley fall in love and for some reason, they had all decided that there could be another one now: her and this good-looking cowboy. She wanted to stomp his boot right now.

Oh yeah, she was not happy at that moment. And yet those eyes dug into her, and then he topped it off with that grin—one that told her he knew exactly what she was feeling.

* * *

Well, he hadn't exactly started the day off right. But he hadn't been able to help himself when he'd come up and all those ladies had greeted him and there she had been, looking beautiful. Abe knew he had goofed up but as he eventually excused himself—better to do that than get bucked on the head or something—he went to his arena, where his fellas were gathered, gearing up for the first horse ride.

Gus had been with the ranch for years but this was his first trip out at the camp. Kurt and Abe's first trip out had been when Tucker McIntyre had asked them to come help them set it up for Riley, and then the romance had begun. He and Kurt had come ever since, off and on, to help out. They had had fun and they had watched Riley and Sophie have their first baby. But before that, they had watched from a distance that Christmas as Riley and Sophie hadn't had a baby, but they had watched their two brothers' wives have them. At the same time, Riley and Sophie *had* announced they were having a baby that year; then low and behold, they were expecting again and this time at Christmas. It was now being thought that every other Christmas, Miss Alice was going to get a grandchild for a Christmas present. It was fun watching this family grow, and he and his buddies were glad to fill in wherever they were needed.

"Hey, dude." Kurt finished tightening a saddle onto the horse Lilly had ridden. "You look kind of like you're having a not so good day." He hitched a brow.

His words drew the attention of Gus, the older man helping him, and he stopped right in his tracks. He was carrying a saddle; he had it set in front of him, holding it with both hands, and he grinned. "So it's been better than just lunch the other day? It's advancing, huh? You know, I think that's what this camp is good for. The fellas who work here fall for a lady camping here. I've been watching all the ladies who've come in, and I don't know about you, but I'm an old dude. I'm pretty much settled in, but there's a lot of ladies my age. And they look like they're having a good time. It's kind of gotten my interest." He laughed.

Kurt looked at Gus. "Hey, don't go looking at me like that. If I decide I want to have a romance, I can. Who knows—it might be my wedding you're coming to next."

"Well, that would be just fine." Abe tried not to laugh but who knew—there were a lot of really great ladies here. It suddenly hit him. "Who are you eyeing?"

he asked Gus. "Connie? No…Maggie—nooo, you've got your eyes on Ida."

As if wondering how he had read Gus's brain, the man stared at him with a big grin. "Now how did you know that? That woman is something. Don't go getting any ideas though. I just noticed her the other night when I was standing guard over here by the firepits. She came over with her buddies and they were talking and I heard it all. She's a nice lady, lost her husband about, well, let's see…I think she said it's been about eight years now. She said the first year they came, it had been about six years and that her and her two buddies had all lost their husbands about that same year. This whole camp here has really helped them, and they have a good time. They get out and about. Kind of made me glad you invited me out here to help. I told you I stayed home a lot and was satisfied staying at the cabin, but I don't know…it's just been one day and I'm already glad I'm here."

Abe knew exactly what he was saying. *Been there, done that.* Age didn't matter. When attraction—although, on his part, he was pretty sure it was more than that—hit you, it just did, like a heavy load of horse feed being slammed into you…somebody was chucking it to you from the back end of the pickup truck, and you weren't looking for it. It whacked you out. It had happened to him a time or two when he was growing up on Sunrise Ranch. He had learned pretty quickly when you were unloading feed to pay attention. But it hadn't quite hit him until just then that, yup, he had been hit by a bag of feed when Lilly, the beauty, rolled down that hill. Lilly wasn't a bag of feed—no way—but the way he'd been affected since he'd gone running after her felt as if he'd been slammed with one.

He'd been watching her at the restaurant, drawn to her, but helping her get up from that sand after her roll down, he was now hooked.

"Look, guys, I've got a problem. I mean, really a problem. I think I'm in love with Lilly. I didn't expect it, but I've been, well, you know, I've been around her…I go eat at the inn just to be near her, but, well, I'm in trouble. She doesn't want any kind of relationship."

Kurt hitched his brow again. "You mean that kiss you gave her the other night wasn't planned?"

"*What*, you saw that?"

Kurt grinned. "Yep. The firepit you were at had had a little trouble and I was coming to check on it and there you two were. I turned away real quick and gave you privacy because you two were kissing like…"

"Like they were in *loooove*," Gus cooed and grinned.

Holy cow, he was in big trouble.

"Come on," Kurt said. "Don't worry. It's going to come out all right. Everything's going to come out just fine. I mean, look at it this way—if it's meant to be, it will be. I don't really know what I'm talking about because I've never been in love, but I'm figuring I should be watching and learning because it's not like I'm not planning on falling in love one day. You, too. You might be wanting to smack me right now but I'm just going to say, if it's meant to be… That's one sweet lady. Everybody likes her, and maybe she just doesn't know you two are meant to be yet. So be cool—go easy, but don't walk away. Don't make her think there isn't anything there. I mean, you know how when we're having to train a horse, we have to kind of just ease into it a little bit? Maybe that's what you need to do—pretend she's a horse."

Gus busted out laughing. "Yeah, I can tell you she *ain't* no horse. However, Kurt might be right about easing into it. It's not like you're going to tame her 'cause she don't look like she needs taming. But maybe if you ease in there, she will fall in love with you without totally realizing it. Then, boom! Happy ending. And a new beginning."

He stared at his buddies, his heart pounding like there was an explosion fixin' to go off inside him. *Could he do what they were saying to do?* She really wanted to leave here and move forward in her life. "But what if she don't want to stay here? What if, by some lucky piece in time and space, she were to fall in love with me, then be mad at me because she wanted to go off and become a famous chef? Say, in New York or somewhere like that. Which she is well talented to do. Dudes, she's beautiful and talented. She could become one of them chefs on television and be a huge hit. People wouldn't be able to get enough of her pretty smile and great food."

Gus's eyes lit up. "Hey, dude, you might have a good idea right there. She could become a star on TV. Heck, I'd watch it just 'cause I know she can cook. I've eaten at that restaurant, and she's helped with all those meals. And you just say it this way…maybe she could get a show—"

"Let's not go there. I'm in trouble here. I don't need to be talking about a TV show—"

"Hold on, buddy." Kurt sounded as if he'd just discovered gold. "Keep y'alls minds open. I'm saying there are possibilities here."

Gus busted in. "She could become a famous chef and live right here on Star Gazer Island. She could be right up there with those cooking shows that do great, and then you and her could live happily ever after."

"Stop." Abe had enough and held his hand up. "Y'all get back to work. Get the horses ready—I'm not asking—I'm telling you. Got it?"

Both guys looked at each other, then at him but didn't move.

"I'm not kidding, you two. I mean it. I like you both a lot, but if you go messing with this like that, I'm going to be *real* mad and you're going to be *real* sad." *TV show*, yes they were joking but they didn't need to be teasing her so he meant what he said—they would answewer to him.

Both men's brows met in shock as he glared at them. It had been a very long time since he was this mad, but if they did something they thought was cute and it upset the woman he knew without a doubt that he loved, then that would be a bad thing.

"Don't go havin' a hissy fit," Gus snapped. "We'll get to work."

"But," Kurt said, "I might come hang out around there while they're cooking." Abe glared at him, and Kurt held up his hand. "Out of interest. I never thought about it until now but who knows, maybe some of these gals have a daughter and if they like me enough, they'll introduce me. Maybe I'll be ready."

Abe's brain spun. "Whatever. Just keep your mouths shut where that is concerned. I have to help get things ready for the cooking lesson, and I hear some voices behind me, so you guys have riders coming. Be careful, and I mean on all fronts."

He didn't wait for them to say okay; he just walked away. He needed to go hide; he needed to walk in the woods all by himself…maybe shout out a little bit because he was in trouble. Big trouble.

CHAPTER THIRTEEN

"Hi, everyone." Lilly smiled at the large group of ladies who stood around the tables, watching her. She needed her nerves to settle down and took a breath. *She could do this.*

"I love to cook and bake, but I've never had an audience, a sweet group of ladies wanting to learn from me. I'm thrilled. When I first got the desire to become a chef, it began by me watching all those wonderful television shows with cooks teaching adults and kids how to create great things. My sweet mother encouraged me and brought ingredients home so that I could make things I'd seen on the shows." She smiled at the memory. "Mom loved eating everything I cooked—I'm sure early on that it wasn't as good as Mom said it was…but the encouragement helped me continue on the path toward becoming a professional chef."

Then, she'd found a young man who told her she was beautiful and wonderful and drew her away from her dream. She'd been distracted from her goals, and her mother had continued to encourage her to focus back on them. When her fiancé had dropped her because he fell for someone else, she was heartbroken and humiliated. Ridiculously, she'd gotten involved with the ex's friend, who had always had a crush on her. So that again had distracted her. Then he dropped her too.

Her sweet mother helped pick her up and encouraged her to think of herself and her dreams and to stop tossing them to the side. She'd finally listened to her mother. Then she was accepted at an elite cooking school and the girl with the yearning heart for love had been sidetracked by a fellow student chef. Once again, he finished before her and left her behind.

It had been hard but after that third one walked away, she went home and apologized to her mother and declared her heart would never get in the way of her career again. The person her mom had always believed she could be would be who she would become. And so here she was, Lilly told herself as she realized she'd paused in talking. She reminded herself once more that nothing would get in the way ever again. And it hadn't.

Now, past worrying about Lilly, her mother had finally focused on her own life; she'd met a wonderful man and they'd flown to meet his family over the holidays. Lilly hoped her mother would be the one to get married.

Lilly smiled, looked out at the ladies and realized she hadn't finished her greeting. "I'm just thinking now how much she would enjoy standing out there among all of you. *This* she would love so much and that makes me happy. *So*, are you ready for teamwork? In the kitchen, we rely on good teamwork to bring spectacular meals to life. And today we're going to bake ten mouthwatering cakes and do them as teams. They'll be our dessert for tonight's dinner and a delicious, rewarding treat to enjoy."

The ladies didn't even hesitate when they had all swarmed in and each took up a spot at a table. Everything they needed was set up, and she was glad that Abe had been so easy to work with after their evening. All the ingredients, the mixers, measuring cups, and, thankfully, ovens had been brought in for class.

She wasn't even sure how or where he had gotten them from, but they were there, waiting and heated up. There were also refreshments, and she planned to talk to them while they waited for them to bake, to answer any questions they had and encourage them to step out and bake more difficult recipes. It was fun; at least, she had always thought it was. And she knew as she stood there that this was going to be fun.

"I am so ready for this." Connie rubbed her hands together before she picked up a copy of the recipe. She, Ida, and Maggie were all together, plus another lady.

Everybody was talking, and Lilly felt a bit silly as she began telling each one of them what to do. They were older and smart, but their clear excitement about making an elegant cake was amazing. New was a good thing.

After everyone was working, she realized that Gus, the older cowboy, was leaning on a pole at the back near the exit. When he caught her eye, he grinned and gave her a thumbs-up. She saw over to the side was Kurt, the cowboy who was Abe's friend and overseeing the horse riding while Abe was overseeing the camp. He leaned on a counter, both his elbows resting on the hard surface as he held his phone between his hands. He looked as if he were reading messages or watching something on his screen. Studying it would be a more accurate description.

Some of the ladies started to laugh, and as she pulled her gaze from him to them, she saw he started to grin, as if his show or message were funny. When her gaze landed on the laughing ladies, she saw they had turned the mixer on and splattered chocolate cake mix across all of their bellies.

"Oh my, having fun, ladies?" She moved over to join in with their laughter. Needless to say, the lady, Clara, was very careful as she set the mixer to going this next time.

They were laughing and enjoying themselves at all the tables as she went around and gave each woman personal attention and answered questions they might have. Many of them were cooks but were obviously open to learning new techniques. When they each had taken turns working on their project, she walked to each table, smiled at each lady, and then, when she had gotten a look at everybody's dish, they walked to the ovens and placed them inside.

"Well, I have to say that was fun and I'm already hungry. All the chocolate and that marshmallow and that buttercream and all that other fancy stuff we added in there…it's going to be fun getting that icing on there when it's time."

Maggie grinned as she bent and looked inside the oven window that was lit. "So, we're going to have to," she stood up, "test everybody's cake and see whose is best. How does that sound?"

One of the ladies stuffed her hand on her hip. "What are you telling me, you think yours is going to be better than mine? Girlfriend, I've been baking all my life and yes, I think this is awesome, but I can guarantee you I added something extra to mine. It's going to be better than anyone else's."

"You added something different than what our

Lilly said to add?" Connie asked, defiantly.

Lilly saw her flashing eyes and stepped in, grinning. "Well, ladies, obviously you have been baking all your lives and to want to change recipes up is a natural thing. I used to do it too. I hope what you added, Ms. Brenda, makes it even better. If it does, you'll have to sneak me the ingredient so I'll know the secret."

Everyone laughed, and so did Brenda. Movement at the back of the room caught Lilly's attention. Gus and Kurt were still there; Kurt hadn't moved from where he leaned on the counter, looking at his phone. *Did the man stay on his phone all the time when he wasn't riding a horse?*

But then she saw Abe standing behind him with a big grin on his face. His cowboy hat was tipped back, his arms crossed, and his long legs were separated in a firm stance while he watched her. Seeing the smile on his face sent bursts of joy through her, fireworks exploding as she met his beautiful eyes.

She grinned. She was enjoying this, and he had helped her get here, despite the kiss. She had to thank him for helping set this up so the ladies could have a new entertaining time at the camp.

She looked around at the happy ladies, excitedly talking as they waited on their creations to bake. And that made her happy. This was fun.

Really enjoyable.

* * *

Abe hadn't meant to go in and watch the baking class. But he hadn't been able to help himself, so here he stood in the back entrance along with Gus and Kurt too, who was leaning against that back counter, busy reading something on his phone. Then the ladies started to laugh, and Gus and Kurt looked at each other and laughed too. For some reason, it seemed odd, so Abe stepped closer and looked over Kurt's shoulder—he was videoing Lilly's class.

What?

He stepped away, put his hands on his hips, and just watched the show. She was really good. She told the ladies that her mother had helped her go for her dream, held on to hope that she would, and now she would soon be a true chef. He found it good that she had the support of her mom.

He couldn't talk about his mom like that. He wished with all of his heart he could have, but his mom had given up after his dad abandoned them and had drunk them into debt. He remembered his dad beating on his mom a few times before he left them. He had never come to terms with how she still wanted him after all he'd done, and she abandoned Abe by immersing herself in alcohol and eventually death—he had already been taken away by then but had found out later.

In his internal anger, he'd been unable to figure out why she had loved his dad despite all he'd done to them. To her, especially.

He didn't think about it often anymore; he'd found life again at Sunrise Ranch. He had been blessed by Nana, the grandmother who ran the kitchen, and her friends from Dew Drop, the town close to the ranch. Those ladies had helped all the boys and shown them what a real woman was made of.

As he stood there, looking at all the ladies surrounding Lilly, his heart kicked up because he'd already connected these ladies with the ones who had helped him, an angry teen, learn what women should be made like. But Lilly…she drew him like no other, and he knew, watching her, that she was happy. These ladies spoke to her too, or something was making her smile like he'd never seen her smiling before.

She was happy. Truly happy as she talked to the ladies about baking.

The class was ending, and he turned and headed for the door, Lilly's smile on his mind as he walked into the sunshine.

Kurt and Gus had followed him out, and that was good. The ladies were talking and having a fun time while they waited on their cakes to bake. They didn't need to be in there in the background, intruding on their time together.

Once outside, he walked away, motioning to the guys to follow him. When they were a good distance away, he turned and looked at Kurt.

"So you want to tell me what you're videoing that for?" he asked bluntly. The idea that Kurt was taping Lilly was odd; maybe he had his eyes on her, and that irritated Abe. He didn't want anyone to set their sights on the woman he hoped to win—stop, he didn't want to go there. He needed to calm down. Lilly was the one who would decide something like that, not him.

Kurt was grinning, and Gus was too. "Abe, she's good. Didn't you see how good she was? Those little ladies were enthralled and happy as she helped them create a cake. She had their attention and when I zoomed in on her, she looked as good standing there teaching them her magic as some of the most famous cooks on television. She had them at her first words and the first stir of that dish."

Abe's mind was boggled. "True, she did. We all saw that she's amazing. I can already tell you her cooking is delicious but yeah, with a group like that, she was magic. She was…who cares about her food?" His words got big grins from his friends.

"You got it right," Gus drawled. "She lets that smile shine, and those gals all dived into creating."

"And it was great to watch on tape," Kurt said.

"*Why* did you video her teaching the class? Are you interested in Lilly?"

Kurt grinned, and his eyes danced. "Dude, remember I saw you kissing her in the moonlight last night."

Relief flooded through Abe. "Then why?"

"Look, I started to mention it before but you got mad so I shut up. My sister is a producer out there in California for a cooking channel. They produce cooking shows of all kinds. You know how Lilly talked about how she watched them growing up and they inspired her? They inspired my sister, too—not to cook but instead to bring cooking shows to life. Now she's out there and produces cooking shows just like she dreamed. Really good ones. He looked from one to the other. "She's looking for a new show. I got to thinking about it and couldn't help myself; I taped it and am going to send the video to her. I've never done this before, but I think she's going to love it. She wanted something different and when I heard how much the ladies were looking forward to this glamping and baking… I thought I'd tape it and send it to her. She can go from there."

Abe was lost—a *cooking show*. "You can't do that

unless you ask Lilly."

Kurt's brows met as he frowned. "You're serious?"

"Yes. If she doesn't want you to send the video, then you won't send it."

Kurt sighed and pushed his phone into his pocket. "Okay, fine. But I don't see anything wrong with it. I will do what you want me to do, but I'm just going to put it straight to you—if I send it, there is a big chance that nothing comes from it. The probability that it happens is small, even as much as we enjoyed watching her and those ladies. So why tell her and chance exciting her and then it falls through? Why not send it, and if my sister loves it as much as we do and is interested, it could be a great surprise. A surprise she can say yes or no to. Think about that." He stared hard at Abe, then hitched a brow.

Abe had seen what Kurt had seen. Lilly had been amazing, and everyone had enjoyed watching her.

But was this right?

"Like he said," Gus drawled, "she'll get the choice in the end, if his sister tries to pick her up for this deal. She'll get the opportunity, if that happens, to say yes or no. But if he doesn't turn it in, then she won't have the opportunity to say yes or no. Besides, we've all seen how quiet she is. Be honest—if he asked her, she'd say no. Because I don't think she's confident enough to expect it to bring back an offer. Anyway, I'd say let him send it in." He grinned broadly. "It's his sister, and I'll tell you, if they offer a show where I can watch her cook—especially with a group of ladies like today—then I think it would be a huge hit." He stared at Abe, challenging him to disagree.

Abe couldn't. He saw it. He actually saw, in his mind, that beautiful, talented woman, who was inspiring all those women who were here to cook something wonderful, doing it on television and everyone enjoying it.

Despite all the things that had been telling him to say *No, no, no*—he let out a sigh. "Send it in. But don't say a word. I have a feeling, if she doesn't like the idea, all three of us can count on her not being our friend anymore. But if she does…then we did right."

That thought sent his whole insides right to the ground, splattering everywhere.

Kurt held up a hand. "Look, I don't want to do this and bring something in between you two. Clearly something good is happening here. Messing that up is the last thing I want to happen."

"She's the one who matters," Abe said.

"Yes, she is," Gus agreed. "You're spot-on, Abe. If this is what her life is meant to be, not that we know everything, but we all know what we saw today—that pretty lady came to life out there today, teaching those other lovely ladies to create something amazing. And I can't wait to eat it at supper. I've got a feeling in my big ole heart that Kurt's sister is going to see exactly what we saw. So, sending it in is what needs to be done."

Abe knew he was right. "I agree. If this is something that can make her into something she's meant to be, which I believe is a famous, amazing chef who the world needs to see, then I can't get in the way. Send it to your sister."

CHAPTER FOURTEEN

Lilly had enjoyed herself so very much in the class. All the ladies had loved it too. And the cakes…goodness, they were beautiful, and she knew they were going to be delicious. Everyone was eager to test them at dinner. It would be fun testing small bites of each cake. She had enjoyed watching the ladies enjoy making the cakes together and hoped tasting would be just as enjoyable.

Now, many of them had left to go ride horses or go to the beach and walk. It was a little cooler today, and she didn't think swimsuits were on the agenda for any of them. However, walking on the beach, riding horses, or sitting at the outdoor areas beside a campfire and visiting, and maybe knitting as she'd heard some of them saying they loved to do. They all had plans before dinner.

She had stayed in the tent to make sure the cakes were all set up and covered so that the ladies could go do their thing—she had secretly hoped Abe would come back inside.

She was stunned by the feeling of pleasure that had ridden through her at the look on his face as he watched her teaching the class. Their gazes had connected, held and her heart had raced in that moment. Later, before he left, he had looked over his shoulder and smiled at her. That smile, that look had made her aware that him thinking she'd done a good job meant something to her, meant more than anything or anybody—other than her mother. And that had made her heart soar. *What was she thinking?*

Now, she'd just walked outside the tent when she saw him walking across the yard. And when he saw her, he stopped walking, put his hands on his lean hips, and smiled.

Heart thundering, she walked his way. The good-looking cowboy's smile and the way his eyes were dancing were a major draw—and she needed to thank him for going along with the ladies on having the cooking class.

"It was amazing," he said before she spoke.

"I loved it," she said, more certain of that than anything she had ever been certain of in her life. "It was the most incredible feeling watching those ladies as they listened to me and did what I showed them. I don't see how they could have had more fun than I did though. These cakes they made are going to be wonderful. They made them exactly the way I said and worked hard at it, but one I can't wait to taste is from the lady who got creative and added her secret ingredient to it."

"Really?"

She grinned. "Yes, and that's where it all begins, bringing your own spunk to the dish—it can be great or not, but it's still a creative step out. So, tonight's meal is going to be fabulous."

His grin was huge as he listened to her.

"I can guarantee you, I'm eager to eat some and so are those other two."

"They looked like they were so interested, and I

think that was great. But I'm not real sure about Kurt. He was on his phone, it seemed like. I didn't stare back there much but he definitely seemed infatuated with something."

Abe looked a little disturbed for a second. "He's fine. He enjoyed it. He was listening the whole entire time. When we went outside afterward to get out of y'alls way to talk, those two were hoping food would start soon so they could eat. The cakes."

She laughed; he had had to add on "the cakes" just to make sure she knew what he was talking about. "Well, I'm sure whatever the food is going to be, it's going to be awesome also. The food last night was amazing."

"They bring it in from all over. But your food is the best, and that's why I come to the inn at least once a week. You're an amazing chef."

He had said he came to eat her food at the inn. She didn't know how to feel about that. She didn't want to get carried away. "Well, I'm going to go see where I can help out right now. I think some of the ladies were going to go have manicures and they told me I should come enjoy one and check out what's going on."

"I think that sounds like a great plan. So, you head on out and I'll see you tonight."

She headed out, all right, as fast as she could, her mind whirling. Her insides went crazy as she tried not to think about…well, not think about what she was thinking about.

* * *

Abe was more than ready when dinner started that night. He, for one, was ready to try all the desserts that she had helped all those ladies make. But the truth was, mostly he was ready to be under this big tent, enjoying the nice band that was going to play tonight. They played really good music, and the ladies enjoyed them every year that they came and—yeah, in his heart of hearts—he hoped he got a dance.

He was a crazy man. She wasn't going to dance with him. And more than likely, he wasn't going to be direct enough or brave enough to ask her because everybody would be there.

All the ladies were excited about her; they all thought she was awesome and wanted to see her be a huge success. They didn't know what Kurt had done, but if him sending off that video were to produce an offer to this sweet cowgirl…no, she wasn't a cowgirl; she was a chef. *What would a chef want to do with a cowboy?* He reeled in his thoughts as he headed out of his camper and, to his surprise, she was walking out of her camper. He had forgotten to check and see whether the coast was clear. But it wouldn't have mattered anyway, because she was opening the door the instant he opened his and there they were, no turning back.

"Well, you ready?" He smiled big—couldn't help it. She looked amazing. She had on white jeans with colorful sandals. His gaze dropped to them, and he saw she had pink toenails. The sandals had three stripes across the top of her foot: one across her toes, one midway, and one across the arch. On each strap was a tiny different colored flower. They were cute—they were adorable—and he yanked his gaze up to her beautiful face. He bypassed her lavender blouse and met those golden eyes, swallowed hard.

Say something. "You look amazing."

She inhaled. "Thank you. I'm excited about tonight. It's been a great three days since I got the invitation— my brain's a little whirly right now so I'm glad I matched up my outfit with my nails." She grinned and waved her pale lavender nails in the air. "I got my manicure and pedicure, as you can see. I had brought these sandals just because we're at the beach and I hadn't worn them yet, so my pedicure made it a good time to do so. I've had an amazing day."

She was talking rapidly; it made him smile. "You look great. And the ladies always talk about how good the gals are who come and do their manicures and pedicures. I'm glad you got to enjoy that. I actually saw Ida afterward, and she said that they all loved you being there. And they're thoroughly excited about the next cooking class." He grinned big. "And they cannot wait to test their dessert tonight. And she said to get you back out on that dance floor. They said you had a really good time last night, even though they thought you looked a little upset about something when you first came in."

He shouldn't have said anything about their kiss,

even though he didn't say, after the kiss, he knew why she was upset-looking when she left. Yes, they'd met before he sent the grocery list to the store and they'd both pretended nothing had happened, so why had he just brought it up again?

"It's been a great day. I still think the kiss was a mistake, standing there in the moonlight—I mean last night."

He put his hands on his hips. "Yeah, it was in the moonlight, all right and it was awesome—" He cut his words off and slapped himself mentally. "Anyway, I didn't mean to intrude, we just won't talk about last night...we'll move forward to tonight. You've contributed something huge and the ladies really enjoyed it."

She looked away. He could tell that that nervousness that she had sometimes was moving in, not the sure and confident chef but the other one, the one that drew him like a magnet. Not because he wanted her to feel like she had no confidence, but because he wanted to be the one who helped her realize how great she was, and not just when she was standing behind a creation that she had made with her hands and her mind and her creativity. He wanted to be the one who helped her realize that everything about her had that in her.

"I did too," she said finally.

"I thought so. Now, may I escort you to your fans, great chef that you are?" He meant every word as her golden eyes held his.

"Let's do this."

He stepped into the path and paused, waiting for her. Then they walked together, not too close, but his arm brushed her arm. Those familiar tingles and electric shots flew through him. This was going to be a great night.

He was going to make certain that it was, although he didn't think there was anything else it could be. Everyone was looking forward to tonight.

* * *

The music started to play just before they reached the door. And as if she had been standing there, waiting for her, Ida came over and flung her arms around Lilly. "It is going to be awesome. All of our cakes are sitting out there, and they just look grand. Even the cooks—well, not the cooks but the servers who are here to feed us our meal—asked who made all the beautiful cakes, and we told them we did…everybody did. We're all excited. As you can tell, we all got here early just 'cause we wanted to see what they looked like sitting on the table over there."

Lilly smiled, still having an arm wrapped around her as she looked at the shorter lady. "I'm so glad that y'all are so happy with the class today. I actually was too, and I wanted to come early to see them sitting there, too, but I made myself not do that." She didn't say that she was glad, because if she had come early, she would have missed stepping out the door and seeing Abe. Yes, seeing him had sent lightning bolts thundering through her like she had never, ever even imagined happening, much less happened to her before.

What was it about this man? she couldn't help but ask. Thank goodness she didn't ask out loud but only to herself. If she started asking things out loud, she would be in major trouble.

When they walked inside, they were swarmed by the ladies. He caught her eye, gave her a little salute with a grin, then turned and headed off, she was sure, to check on everything. And she looked at all the ladies who were telling her how much they had had fun today baking those cakes and she felt… Her heart swelled; she felt perfect. She felt as if she were in the right spot at the right moment.

"Ladies, I'm so thrilled that y'all had so much fun today. And I know we can't wait to eat it, but I have to say that I honestly don't know if I've ever had so much fun before. I thank all of you."

Their faces took on a look of disbelief. Every one of them, either their mouths dropped open, their eyes got wide, or they gasped.

Maggie was the first one to say anything. "You are wonderful. So here's the deal: you gave us such a great day, so we're very thrilled that we gave you a great day. But, girlfriend, we are fixin' to have a great night. Last night, yes, we know you came and danced with us, and you had a good time, but we all know that you were not completely with us. You had that sad look on your face when you first came in, but tonight you have a great look on your face." Her eyes twinkled and her glance shifted to where Abe had walked to the tables across the room and back. "We think that tonight's going to be one of the best nights we've ever had when we come here to this wonderful camp."

"That's exactly what we're hoping." Connie walked up and threw an arm around her waist, giving a sideways hug. "You, girlfriend, have what it takes to become one of us, which we hope you do. *Well,* the truth is, we kind of want you to join but not really. You see, the majority of us have had the loves of our life involved in our life and then we lost them. And we know what that feels like. We just want you to be a part of us right now, but we want you to have what we used to have—a man to love and who loves you deeply like you deserve. Thank the good Lord He gave us Sophie to start this group up and give us the fun that we have, but we're all glad she's living her dream life and growing her family. And we hope you do too."

Ida stepped up. "Sophie and that sweet husband of hers knew exactly who to pick to fill in for them when they were going to be out. I'm not sure if you realize that but somehow or another, she knew that you would fit in with us. And that we would *love* to bake. But I think she also knew something else that we can all see… Anyway, let's not get off on that. I don't want you to get upset tonight. We are going to have a good time, aren't we, everybody?"

All the ladies cheered and then they led her along, deeper into the tent. Music played as they headed toward the food line.

"You'll sit with us." Ida tugged her in line with her, Connie, and Maggie.

Lilly chuckled. "Ladies, I think that's part of my job—making sure I do everything I can to help you have a good time, so if that means eating with you, then I'm all in." That got her a hoot of laughter, and she was thrilled she'd made a fun joke.

"But you're going to dance with someone else." Connie nudged her arm and nodded toward something.

She followed the nod; it was shot to the other side of the table, where Abe stood talking to the cooking team. It hit her in that moment that these ladies obviously had matchmaking on their mind and tonight...tonight she wasn't going to take their joy away. That was her job and, honestly, she needed an excuse to have fun and let these crazy emotions chugging away inside her have a little space.

CHAPTER FIFTEEN

be caught the ladies obviously saying something about him to Lilly, tuning in to his curiosity. That wasn't the first time he had gotten those looks from the ladies, but he had a feeling that tonight was going to be really interesting. The seating was all throughout one area of the large tent; then there was their large dance area up front, where the singer was already entertaining as everyone ate. He, Gus, and Kurt took a seat with the other fellas helping with the horse riding. Some of them had never been here before either.

Toby was a cowboy a little younger than Kurt and was really good at what he did, but Kurt had thought he would be a good one to add to the list of helpers. Then there was Trey, who was middle-aged. He was nowhere near the age of Gus but he wasn't Abe's age either; he was in between. And he was a good man. So, they had a little bit larger group of guys helping with the riding this year because the camping group had grown too. With more help, they could have the riders riding and give Gus and Kurt some time off. They could also give him more people around to help him out if he needed it. And as he looked around, he felt all the fellas were having a good time.

It also gave Gus and Kurt some extra free time for them to do what they'd done earlier today, watching the gals bake and making a video that he was still nervous about.

"They are really loving this place. I'm a little surprised." Toby sat between Abe and Gus. Kurt sat on the other side of Abe, and then the others filled in the other spots, but the four of them had a great shot of the room.

"These ladies love it. I'm sure you've met Ida, Maggie, and Connie. They were the three who helped Sophie get this started. And since she's not as involved in it now, they've helped take over running the group."

Gus leaned forward and grinned real wide. "Well, that's good because I hope they wait and deliver the baby on Christmas. The McIntyres have a new fad going, have babies on Christmas but skip a year like they did last Christmas and then have another one like is expected this year. But wouldn't it be cool if they had another baby on Christmas like they did the year before?"

Toby chuckled. "That would be cool. I've been working for the McIntyres for several years, and I never expected to see those brothers marry off so quickly. I mean, it was like dominos once Jackson married Nina first and then one by one, they rolled down that hill—or they would say, rolled up a hill. They're all happy. Even Dallas, who I never thought I would see marry. Now, he's got two babies and is smiling all the time. It's pretty cool."

"You going to copy them soon?" Gus asked, grinning bigger.

Abe wanted to laugh because he knew what was coming.

"Ha! You know I ain't ready for that. I'm not in the

mood for getting tied up with anybody. But that sweet lady and that little baby Dallas rescued on that beach and changed his heart—well, for me it would have to be something like that. Love would have to slam me off a cliff before I thought I was ready. Do you agree, Abe?"

Everyone laughed, and Abe was startled to be pointed out. But internally he agreed, because he was the one who had just gotten knocked off the cliff by his feelings for Lilly. And he was struggling in the waves and rocks right now.

Kurt, on the other side of him, grunted. "Oh yeah, tell us, Abe, don't you agree?"

Abe wanted to stand up and walk away. His gaze, though, instantly shot across to that beautiful Lilly, who was as surrounded by matchmaking ladies as he was by cowboys. She leaned back and laughed with delight at something one of the ladies said, and he couldn't help wonder what was getting them all so tickled. All he knew was he liked it; he liked seeing her happy like that.

"*Well,* aren't you going to answer?" Gus drawled real slow, drawing Abe's gaze as he hitched an eyebrow.

"Come on, y'all can see she's beautiful and it's

obvious I'm really attracted to her, more than I've been attracted to anybody. But she's got plans—dreams—and they don't involve a cowboy from Corpus Christi."

"You ain't from Corpus Christi; you're from Sunrise Ranch in Dew Drop, Texas," Kurt pointed out. "And from everything I've heard from you, that place is a great place for fellas who had nobody to find their way. I've heard you talk about it a few times and now I'm thinking you're on the verge of falling in love. Finding your way to what your life is meant to be. I've been watching."

Abe had no words, but all the cowboys stared at him. "Y'all…okay, he's right. I've never felt what I feel for that amazing lady sitting over at that table. But in all honesty, I don't want to get in her way. I keep saying that and it's true. I want her to be the success she dreams of being. In my book, she's already there but it's her book, her mind and heart that matters. I can't say more but she has a past, too. A past that drives her to achieve what she needs to achieve. I can't get in the way."

Kurt placed his hand on his shoulder and squeezed. "Dude, we all follow everything you do, and we can tell you that you are one good fella. I'm not the smartest one sitting here but I'm going to say, let your heart lead you. Like I said before, if it's meant to be, it's meant to be. I can say this, from what I saw today when she was teaching that class and she looked up and saw you standing there while she was teaching—and I got it on video, so I'm just going to tell you—when people see that video and she's looking at the video with love in her eyes, it ain't the video she's looking at. It ain't the food the people watching the video are going to think she's talking about. Nope, it's you. You, Abe, were standing right behind me, and it was you she was looking at."

"Yep," Gus said. "I saw it too. It was you who was standing there and her gaze was locked to. Those gold eyes lit up like Christmas lights. I ain't never seen them do that before. So, fellas," he looked around at the table of guys as Abe's heart stampeded inside his chest, "I think tonight is a night to change things up on this dance floor. Those ladies like to dance by themselves but tonight, I say we all join in. I bet you they welcome us. And maybe if this dude will get up the courage, it will give him an excuse to ask that sweet Lilly to dance."

Abe knew it was a great plan, and he was all in.

"Gus," Kurt laughed, "you've got a great idea. I have a feeling that those ladies we've all come to know will welcome us to do that, because they're trying to set these two up too. So, when the dancing starts, let's get the party started."

Abe's pulse blasted as all eyes of his buddies around the table rested on him. And unable to help it, he grinned. "Sounds like a plan. I'm all in."

He just hoped he wasn't messing up. After all, if he was never going to get to hold her in his arms again, at least tonight he'd have a chance to hold her close and let his heart say goodbye.

* * *

She was having a good time; Lilly couldn't deny it. These ladies were so funny, and oh yes, she knew they had plans for her tonight. She wanted to deny them, but she knew that if somehow, someway, if she got the chance to dance with Abe, she would do it.

The thought had her mind whirling, as the need to run from him and the need to run to him were having a duel. But she knew tonight she just couldn't walk away. Thank goodness it was cake time first.

"All right." Connie rose and addressed the tent full of people. "Y'all ready to grab us some of that cake before we get out there on that dance floor and have ourselves a good time?"

That was all it took. In an instant, everyone headed to the dessert tables, as did everyone at Lilly's table. She, Ida, and Maggie, along with the other three ladies at their table, followed Connie as she strode across the room toward the tables.

As they passed Abe's table, she saw he was grinning—yes, her gaze had been drawn to his instantly, drawn with no option. At least she took in that all the guys were smiling too so she yanked her attention away from all of them and followed her group.

They reached the tables, every lady gathered at the cake that they had helped make and the slicing began. They had already told them to put some big plates at the table—not the little dessert plate, but a big one. And they sliced small pieces and laid them on everybody's plate.

"I hope y'all enjoy mine with the extra addition to it," Brenda drawled as she grinned widely. The short lady was very proud. They had laid the pieces of cake out in a row, just like the cakes were lined up so everybody knew which one was hers—the third piece on the plate.

Chuckles rose up from everyone. They were all actually looking forward to testing out her secret ingredient, and so was Lilly. Anything was going to be exciting to get her mind off the cowboy walking toward her. She had had to move on down the line, getting her cake, and the other ladies were moving slow, but they had all designated one of their ladies to be the main slicer. Ida was the one at the main table, and then they went on down so slowly everyone was moving down the line.

As Abe reached Connie standing there with her plate, she handed it to Abe. "Here you go, Abe. You two go off and test those cakes, then come back and tell us which one you thought was best—then y'all get out there on that dance floor. Oh and remember…let us know how number three is on the secret ingredient, 'cause if it's good, we're all going to want to know what it is. But I already snuck a little taste and the one that you helped us make is amazing, so I can't even imagine something making it better."

Even though she was disturbed that she and Abe were being sent off on their own adventure, she was relieved they weren't being pushed to the dance floor just yet. She grinned. "Connie, in this industry, you learn that a single ingredient makes the recipe yours. That means what she did, if it's really good, is now her own recipe; it just has another ingredient in it. Believe me, I worked a lot of times figuring out my secret ingredients, and now y'all know them. Well, I haven't said which one in my recipe is the secret ingredient but y'all know my recipe now, that's how much I love y'all." Yeah, her words had come from her heart.

Connie's sweet eyes glistened as she reached in and gave her a hug around the waist since she was holding a plate. "Believe me, girlfriend, we all love you. Now you two go off and have a good dessert. And please tell us.

I can guarantee you, I'll be experimenting with my own secret ingredient in recipes."

They were grinning as they turned and started to a table. But she realized that the tables they were coming back to were full.

"How about we go out to that first seating area outside and we test out these cakes?" Abe said, his voice low so nobody around might hear him.

Her insides trembled. "Sure, lead the way." And so she followed him out the entrance and to the first firepit. There he waited for her to take a seat, standing beside her, she assumed he was making sure if she tripped with a plate in one hand he'd catch her. The idea was actually tempting but she shoved it away and sat down carefully.

And then he sat down beside her in the chair that gave them a little space in between. The chairs were always set up to where there were several of them but walking room in between. She suddenly couldn't decide whether she was glad for the space or whether she wished they were closer. If they'd made it to the dance floor they would have been in each other's arms right now—

I'm in trouble.

Yes, you are. "So," she blurted out needing to get her mind where it belonged. "All of them on that plate are from my recipe. The first one is from Ida, Connie, and Maggie's table. And then the other ones are from all the other ladies' tables. The third piece is the one with the added ingredient. I hope they're all *really* good—"

His plate sat on his knees, his fork in his hand as he grinned at her. His eyes sparkling in the firelight—making her heart jitter-bug in response—dance floor or no dance floor.

She forced her next words. "…I hope they're perfect."

"They're all going to be good and I'm going to enjoy each piece." And with that, he took a large forkful of the first one piece from which he'd pulled the fork. Everybody's forks were stuck in the first piece on their plates then all the others pieces of cake were laid where their icing faced the same direction so they would know to go from the first one to the one that's icing was closest. Going in that direction would show which table of ladies baked the cake. That had been some heavy-duty instructions that Connie, Maggie, and Ida had come up with. But it worked.

She watched as he pulled the fork from his mouth and started to chew. This was one of her favorite cakes to bake—well, one of the first that she had developed to meet her standards. The first time she had served it, she enjoyed all the compliments that followed. Once there had been a food critic who reviewed this cake and to her shock, it had been a great review. That had thrilled her. And now, as she watched Abe's eyes and the smile come across his mouth as he chewed, her own smile bloomed wide.

"You like it?" she asked softly.

He nodded, still chewing slowly as if savoring its taste. "Oh yeah," he then said. "I like it a lot. I'm telling you, all the times I've eaten at the inn, I haven't had this. Didn't see it offered."

"When I first came up with it, we served it, and then sweet Lisa, the wonderful chef that she is, told me to save it, to keep it in my heart and save for when I open my own restaurant. That it should be my main beginning dessert. And so, I have—not that I'm sure when or if I'll have what it takes to ever open my own place, but if so I'll do as Lisa suggested."

He set his fork down to finish chewing as he swallowed; he wiped his mouth with his napkin. "Wow, Lisa started encouraging you to get ready for your own place from the very beginning? She knew talent when she saw it. *Sees it, taste it.* From everything I know, that woman traveled the country—the world—taking classes and lessons after all that stuff that happened to her because of that creep she was married to. But…" He paused, and then he reached out and placed his hand on hers, which was on the edge of the seat.

Her pulse raced but no words came out as they looked at each other.

"Lilly, do you see how everybody knows you are so talented? You can have and do whatever you choose to do. All these ladies here have been through hard times—they've loved and lost but keep on fighting and moving forward. In reality, kind of like you. One step at a time is all it takes for you to make a dream come true. Yes, you can take one step, then you take another one, and you get sidetracked as you know…but you fall off your horse, you get up and you do it again. Then, the next time, you'll make another stride. As much as I want to tell you—" He stopped.

"Please," she blurted out. "tell me what you were going to say. I need to know."

They stared at each other, the cakes forgotten. Even though they all had to be delicious, right now *this* was more important.

He stood, looking disturbed, and she rose beside him. "I need to get back to work but, Lilly, you are meant to be a chef. You are amazing, and Lisa realized that early on. She's fantastic, too, and knows you have the world waiting for you any way you want it. And I agree." He swooped his lips in and brushed her cheek with a brief touch, and then he walked away.

And Lilly wilted to the chair. She sat there and watched him disappear into the night as a soft song of love drifted through the breeze from the party in the tent. Someone was dancing but it wasn't her and Abe.

CHAPTER SIXTEEN

It was horse riding time again, and Abe didn't know whether to look forward to it or not. Ever since they'd talked he'd known he needed to pull back and had walked away before he said something he shouldn't.

He'd had to. He knew she wanted to be a chef and didn't want him interrupting her path. So, he didn't, wouldn't.

It was already going to be tough, and he didn't want to get any more involved, but today was his day to be with the horse group. If he pulled out, everybody would know. That meant he had to do this, get through it and make it to Saturday.

Once she drove away, the Christmas holiday started; he would hole up in his cabin, herd some cattle when he needed to, and he would *not* eat at Star Gazer Inn ever again. He wouldn't be able to see her and know he could never have her. Not that he believed she would be there much longer. Her dreams were going to come true.

He would cheer her on, knowing that all she wanted would be there for her because she deserved it.

He had just finished helping Gus and Kurt saddle up all the horses when he saw Lilly coming across the area between the horses and the camp. She was surrounded by her group, and behind them was the larger group that would make it a group of twelve. He, Gus, and Kurt would be riding with them; the other cowboys had taken other ladies out earlier.

They liked at least three cowboys with the group just in case something unexpected happened, and they could make sure everyone was kept safe. That's why they did several rides a day.

Now, baking classes were all over, the second one as great as the first, a huge success. As he stood there, looking over the saddle on the horse's back and watching Lilly heading this way, his hand gripped the saddle horn tight. He socked himself in the gut with his invisible fist, telling himself to get his life straight. This was not going to be about him. It was going to be about getting this sweet lady *her* dream.

"You're going to pull that saddle off that horse if you keep holding onto that saddle horn so tight." Gus strode over from where he'd saddled his last horse.

"Look, Gus, is it that obvious that I'm in trouble? I don't need everybody to know."

Gus stuffed both of his hands on his hips, and his eyes grew serious. "It's obvious. But come on, dude, I'm going to tell you, like Kurt and everybody was telling you the other night before the dance—don't give up on this. At least, don't push it, and have a good day today. Give *her* a good day. 'Cause, I can tell you from my own experience, when she leaves and goes on to be a chef, if that's what she intends to do, you want her memories of you to be good." Gus swallowed hard; his gaze melted. "You want there to be a place in her heart for you where there's a future for you two."

"There isn't."

"Don't be angry, or a loser. Encourage yourself too,

not just her. Because, who knows…even if she goes away, she might come back. But if you're not the man you really are, she might not. Anyway, I've got to go. I see Ida coming, and I know who I'm going to be riding with and protecting today." He winked, then strode off.

As Abe watched him head over to the fence post and wave at the ladies, Abe let everything the old man had said sink in. Something told him that that cowboy had regrets that he didn't want Abe to have. And for that, Abe appreciated it…just wasn't sure what to do with it.

He let go of the saddle horn, stepped away, and stepped out into the open area, then past the horses and toward the ladies.

Gus beat him. "You ladies are sure lookin' good today."

They all smiled at the man. Kurt came up from where he had been on the other side and stood beside Abe.

"They do, don't they." He grinned at Abe, elbowed him in the side.

"Yes, they do." He was determined to do what Gus

had told him, and he knew he was going to have Kurt watching.

At movement in the background, he glanced toward the main buildings and saw all the other cowboys watching from afar. Everybody was watching to see how this horse ride started out. They all seemed to have noticed that things hadn't been the same since the night they'd gone to sit by the fire tasting cakes and he hadn't returned to the party or the dance floor. He knew all the women saw it too.

He reminded himself that his job was to make sure this group of ladies had a great time, not for him to have the romance of a lifetime.

Not for him to fall in love and have a happily ever after.

What had he been thinking?

"Ladies," he greeted them, stepping forward, determined to do his job. "We have your horses ready. It's a beautiful day, so let's have fun. Pick your horse and we'll get started as the rest of the group arrives."

His gaze met Lilly's. He touched the tip of his hat with his fingers—a hello in cowboy language—then he moved forward and started to greet the other ladies with actual words. He could ride a horse with this group of ladies; there was nothing that said he had to ride beside Lilly. She had her group that she had become well loved by; he could hang back and give them space.

He would make sure nobody got hurt, and if he happened to see a porpoise or a sea turtle surface out in the water, he'd point it out to everyone. He would stay at the back, keep to himself other than pointing things out, and maybe by the time they finished the hour-long ride, everybody would know that romance wasn't going on between them.

He'd walked away and it was the hardest thing he'd done, and he wasn't backing down. Nothing was between them…except different futures.

* * *

"Isn't this so fun?" Maggie declared from where she was riding beside Lilly, up at the front of the group. Lilly had made certain that she rode wherever Abe wasn't, and as if he were on the same wavelength, he was riding all the way at the back of the group.

She had claimed her same little Bucky and despite this only being the second time she'd ever ridden a horse, she'd been happy to see that Bucky was as easy to ride as he'd been on her first ride. She'd climbed right into his saddle and led the way as Maggie joined her. Everyone else rode behind in groups, with Kurt closest to the right side, and a bit farther back on the left side of the group of ladies was Gus. She smiled, seeing that he made sure he was riding beside Ida. Something wonderful could be blooming there.

She glanced over her shoulder to see whether they were still looking content riding beside each other, and her traitorous gaze went straight back to Abe. He was at the rear, but he was chatting with the last two ladies, who were riding in their saddles turned so they could look at him as they rode.

As always, he was smiling, talking, and getting chuckles from them. And she instantly faced forward and told herself to keep herself looking that way. Looking anywhere but over her shoulder.

That smile of his floated in the air in front of her.

She tried to focus on the curve of the beach, and the beautiful water rolling in drew her attention. Thankfully, because she needed something to dim that smile. It reached inside of her and tugged, pulled, and had her insides shaking.

The thought of leaving to pursue her dream and leaving him behind wasn't sitting well inside her. And just that brief look at him and his smile didn't help. He looked good.

How would he look when she was gone? Was he just able to hide his feelings better than she could? Maybe he didn't feel the deep love that she knew she felt for him.

Every ounce of her felt he loved her. *And if so, would she be able to leave the man who could possibly fulfill her dream by just being the man she loved?* The man her heart had been searching for all these years and made mistakes three times until now. *Would he wait for her to fulfill her dream?*

Questions filled her.

No.

No, she didn't want him waiting on her. She just

wanted him to be happy. And as much as it hurt thinking about it, she wanted some wonderful woman to walk in and win his heart, totally and completely. That way, her walking away wasn't ever a pain to him.

Boy, just the thought of that made her stomach churn.

"You sure are quiet."

She glanced over at Maggie. "I'm, uh, enjoying this."

"Oh yeah? I don't see that. Despite how pretty it is today and how the temperature is perfect, not too hot and not too cold." She laughed. "You don't have to ride up here with me. Why don't you just kind of drift back to the back end and ride with those ladies who are talking to that good-looking cowboy? Or better yet, just ride beside him and take over the conversation."

"Come on, Maggie. Don't go there. I'm having a good time." It was a point-blank lie, and she was so sorry.

Connie moved up beside them from where she'd been behind them, obviously listening. So now she had Connie on one side and Maggie on the other. Lilly looked from one to the other. *Oh goodness.*

"I saw you glance back there. Why don't you just go back there and ride? You two could talk or something. It's just too beautiful a day to waste on…well, I'm going to stay out of it. Sorry about that. You two are going to do what you two are going to do."

And about the time she said that, a small wave rolled in where they rode near the water, and on that wave was, of all things, a huge stingray!

It flipped out of the water with its large, flat body flying in the air, its long, slick tail trailing behind it. Instantly, it startled all three of their horses.

In that second, Maggie's horse reared up; Connie's horse did the same and Lilly's little Bucky just took off at a full-blown charge that almost threw her out of the saddle. But she managed to hang on to the saddle horn with both hands.

Heart racing, blood pounding with each step of the horse's hooves in the sand, she held on harder as they entered the waves along the sand. Gasping for breath, Lilly chanced a look over her shoulder and saw, thank goodness, that Kurt had raced to help Connie, and Gus had charged to save Maggie.

That left Abe as the man who could help her, far at the back of the whole group, and as her little horse raced faster than she could have ever imagined, she knew she was in trouble.

No more time to look back, she leaned forward and clung to the saddle horn as she slipped from one side. She would have yanked on the reins, but she'd dropped them and had no control.

And this little horse that had seemed so tame was clearly terrified by stingrays, so all she could do was hang on.

And pray.

* * *

Abe's heart flew to his stomach when he saw what happened at the front end of the riders. He instantly signaled Ringo to charge, thankful that despite the fact that they were riding on sand, he always made sure he brought his well-trained stallion to ride. In an instant they raced past the screaming ladies. They passed Gus, then Kurt, and he leaned forward and urged Ringo onward.

Thankfully, Lilly was hanging on. She was doing good. With as little riding skills as she had, one thing was for sure: she knew how to hang on.

The feet between them raced away, and he called her name. She glanced over her shoulder just as she tilted to the side, and thank goodness, he was close. Leaning out as his horse raced to her side, he snagged her around the waist and pulled her onto his lap. Heart pounding, he hugged her close as he eased his horse to a trot—no need for him to do it as this smart animal hero knew exactly what to do and was as graceful as a white cloud settling calmly over them.

Lilly had her arms around him; he glanced over his shoulder and realized how far away they were from the others. They were waving, thrilled and happy that he had reached her and now held her.

"I've got you," he said, his own breath hard to get under control, just from worry for her. She was trembling, and he knew why. That was horrifying, but at least it had been on sand and not hard ground.

"Thank you. I didn't know what to do. My reins

were dragging. All I did was hang on to that saddle horn and pray you'd be able to get to me. Because I knew you were the only one who could help me."

His heart swelled with that knowledge. Even though he knew it was only because she knew how good of a rider he was. Unable to help himself, he gave her a gentle hug. One shoulder was against him; her other shoulder was surrounded by his arm, and she lifted that hand and placed it on his heart. As she looked at him, time stopped for him. He looked into those eyes, those golden eyes, and his heart clinched tight. In those eyes, he saw sunrises and sunsets, and with all of his heart, he wanted to be able to look at those eyes when he woke up in the morning…and before he went to sleep at night.

His heart tightened harder, and he fought off emotion. "I need to get you back. Everybody's worried about you."

Her hand that had been resting on his heart now grasped his shirt and scrunched it into her fist. "Abe, my life has been a mess." Her eyes searched his and dug in deep. "It's not you. You are wonderful…"

He heard the tears in her words, saw them in those

eyes before she leaned her forehead against his shoulder.

Tense, he gently rubbed her arm. "Lilly, I need you to know why I'm trying to let you go. Because I love you—" His words broke off as she lifted her head and looked him in the eyes.

Her eyes shadowed in that moment. "I…" She paused then visibly forced forward through gritted teeth, gruff with emotion. "I need to go ahead and leave camp."

His heart that had been on a rampage now shut down with the force of a slamming steel door. "Leave today?"

"Yes. I have really messed up."

Messed up—without even worrying about anybody else behind them, he urged his horse to start walking as he held her firmly in place.

It was time for them to talk.

From behind him, he heard Kurt shout out, "Y'all okay?"

He didn't even look back. "We're fine. We're going around the bend. Y'all head on back."

And he knew that's exactly what his friends would do. Lilly said nothing as they rode, her shoulder pressed against his chest, her head no longer leaning against him but looking forward so it made her lips farther away from his—and that was a good thing because he wanted to kiss her.

He wanted to show her that he *loved* her, that he didn't want her to go.

But no kissing allowed right now. They just had to talk.

He needed to tell her how he felt, and he needed to know why he saw in her eyes that she wanted something more. But her words and actions didn't match up.

And you needed to walk away, demanded his hard-willed mind and heart that had lived through loss of love from his mom and dad and had hardened against it so he could do it again.

For her, if that was what she really wanted.

But did she really want that? Why did her eyes say one thing and her words say another?

CHAPTER SEVENTEEN

Lilly's heart battered her insides top to bottom as she tried to not let her emotions take over. She rode as stiff as she could against this man.

They were going to talk, and she knew it was time to be truthful with him. He needed to know that it wasn't his fault; he needed to know that she had been hurt. "You're right." She looked at him as he brought the horse to a halt. "We do need to talk. I just need to let you in on everything."

"Glad to hear it. Let me help you down." With that, he placed his hands beneath her armpits and slid her off his lap, down to where her feet touched the ground. When she stood on her own feet, he lifted his leg over the horse and dropped down beside her. Then he dropped the reins and stepped away from her.

She needed to get control of herself, but she was never in control except in the kitchen. So, she strode to the edge of the water, not caring whether her tennis shoes got wet or not; she just needed space for a minute between her and Abe.

As if he knew that or needed the same, he walked to the edge of the water but about five feet between them. They looked at each other but he said nothing.

Her world spinning, she forced words out. "It's not you. I told you I messed my life up three different times. Three. I put my career aside and my mom's dreams for me to the side. I messed up when it came to that, to thinking I was in love. I told you how I hurt my mom because she was my number-one fan and gave up so much, hoping that I'd make my dream come true. I have to make that dream come true. I can't let myself get sidetracked again." She raked a hand through her hair and stared out at the water.

Her heart was on a rampage. She knew he wasn't like the other three men. She had been younger; it'd been about two and a half years since she'd concentrated diligently on her career. Before she had taken on this job at Star Gazer Inn, she had worked at two different restaurants, but she had heard about Lisa, the talented chef opening the restaurant. She hadn't hesitated; she'd come and applied instantly. And now here she was.

"I'm not like those other three. I know a treasure when I see it."

A treasure. His words rang through her, made tears well up inside her. She fought hard not to let them appear and dribble down her face. She had to be strong.

"And I see a treasure in front of me, and like you want me to do, I'm going to let you go."

"Abe, one day you'll find someone else. Someone who can love you like you deserve to be loved, when you're ready to be loved. Just make sure it's someone who will put you first like you deserve to be. Honestly, Abe, your parents didn't put you first. You had those wonderful people at Sunrise Ranch and Dew Drop, Texas, thank the good Lord, who gave you what you deserved. I had my wonderful mom. She wanted my dream to come true and worked hard to make it happen. I'm going to be a top chef."

"You are a top chef," he said, his words emotion-free but firm.

"Yes, but, Abe, you deserve someone who will have time to show you how much you mean to her. You deserve so much more than I'll be able to give you once I take the job of my dreams. You are an amazing man and will be an amazing dad. Just you talking about helping those boys who came after you at that ranch—just think how you'll be with a child of your own." *Oh, what an amazing father he would be.* She was letting him go so he could have it all.

He sighed, staring out at the ocean.

She fought off wanting to reach for him. "You'll love your family with all your heart and be loved the same. You deserve that, Abe. But that's not me. My heart is in the kitchen, making food that everybody will love and enjoy. Giving them what my mother knew I could give and worked so hard to help me achieve." She raked a hand through her hair again and yanked her eyes from his.

Those eyes that penetrated through her and softened as she spoke.

She did not need to see his amazing eyes soften.

She stared at the waves, tried to let it bring peace to her as it came in and went out. She faced him. "You were there when I baked with the ladies. You were there, watching those sweet ladies…their excitement completely filled me with joy, because I knew that I had helped produce that joy." Her heart pounded and her words clogged in her throat.

"You were meant to be there," he said. "I saw it. Gus and Kurt…we all saw, as did all those ladies, that's what you're meant to do. And I get that. But all you're saying about me is you seriously don't think you have room in there for a guy who's lost his heart to you. Lost it totally and completely. But I'm going to just say finally, no matter what you say, it's irreversible. I will always love you, whether you are here with me or out there making everyone else smile with your talents."

Tears came, rolled out of both eyes and down her cheeks. She slapped them off her face and sucked in a deep breath. "Abe, you deserve better. Again, you *deserve* someone who can give you everything you have a right to and need. I must finally fulfill this dream that my mom has for me—"

The words hung in the air. Her *mother's* dream.

It used to be *her* dream too.

But those words now hung between her and Abe. She gasped, "I need to go. I need to go back and pack up."

And then she turned and started to walk, almost running down the beach, but she fought for control and didn't run.

She just needed to get away. Get alone.

She needed to think. But with every step she took, those words spun in her head.

Abe held back and didn't say anything as he fell into step beside her. His horse came to him, and he took the reins, letting it walk between them, giving them both a little cushion.

They walked all the way down that beach, with those gentle waves rolling in the only sound around them.

She couldn't talk. She needed space. She needed

room to figure out what her next move would be. She needed space to figure out whether her dream was still her dream…or was it her *mother's* dream?

Oh, how she was confused, mixed up totally in a place she had not expected to be. And yes, there was that knowledge—in her heart of hearts, she had already admitted it—and now she knew it was so true: she loved him.

But in her mind, it had always been that if you loved someone, you gave up your dreams for them. She'd done it three times.

That number three…it was odd: in her life, three fellas had been mistakes. Now, there were three lovely ladies who made a huge difference in her life. Well, those three but also the ladies at the inn and Sophie knowing that Lilly needed to be here at this camp.

As she walked through the sand and the water lapped at her feet, she wondered how Sophie had known she was the one. She had just known that she needed to get out of the walls of a room she loved…she needed time out of the kitchen so that she could see everything.

It suddenly slammed into her. Sophie and Lisa and Alice knew she needed to get out of the walls surrounding her and see things around her.

Had they been right?

As the question rammed into her, they made it back to the camp, walking and not talking.

* * *

Abe had kept his heart closed, and his mouth closed. He wanted her to have what she wanted. He repeated it over and over in order to make it happen.

He knew he would love her for the rest of his life and that he wasn't like those other three men—the jerks who tried to steal her dream from her then walked away. He wasn't like them; he loved her. He never thought he'd love anybody like he loved her. She thought it was just these few days but in his heart of hearts, he felt as though he'd fallen in love with her sitting at that little table at that restaurant. Sitting there, watching through that window as she made dessert. Some would say love at first sight, but it was not first sight; it was watching the joy that radiated from her as she did what she loved. And he *wasn't* taking that from her. No way.

He would just move forward, as he'd always done. He had moved forward after the fiasco with his mother and dad, and he learned true grit, hard determination to let go and move on.

He'd learned to open his heart because of all the other boys who had come to Sunrise Ranch and needed what he had learned he could give: riding horses, working through heartache with work, and focus on moving forward. Always moving forward.

And that was exactly what he planned to do again.

He was a cowboy, a rancher, and he loved his life.

She was a chef; her delight came in making people smile as they ate the wonderful things she made, and she needed that. And he would let her have it. He would just hold on to how he felt, keep it to himself because he couldn't let go of that love. He could just show it by letting her go.

And watching her fly high from a distance…

* * *

Her heart still pounded but finally as they rounded the last sand dune, the one she'd toppled from, camp came into view.

Relief flowed through her as the horse arena was there to the right, but she didn't head that way; Abe would take Bucky so no worries there. Lilly walked faster, headed toward the main camp, then halted as her gaze spotted the crowd.

"What's going on?" she asked as he stopped beside her.

Between the main tent and the snack bar was a van, and standing around it were all the ladies and the cowboys. Kurt, the tall cowboy, stood out as he stood beside a tall, thin female. She wasn't quite as tall as him but close. She was talking; everybody was listening, and Kurt was grinning.

"I'm not sure but obviously something's going on," Abe said.

"It doesn't look like something bad has happened since they're all smiling. So that's a relief." She meant it. She looked at him, then forced her feet to move, and she headed forward.

* * *

Abe didn't know what was going on but at least he was glad to have a distraction from the trauma that was bolted in between the two of them. "Take care," he called, and she looked over her shoulder and nodded. He then continued toward the arena; then he stopped. Reality slammed and he spun to look at the crowd standing around Kurt and the tall woman beside him.

Surely not. He squinted. She looked like Kurt. He dropped the reins and stalked as fast as possible to catch up to Lilly. He had to get to her.

That was Kurt's sister. Surely she hadn't gotten on a plane and flown out here after watching that single, yeah, single but amazing video.

He reached Lilly about fifty feet away from the crowd. "Lilly, maybe I need to walk with you."

She stopped walking and looked toward him. "Why? Is something wrong—do you know something I don't know?"

What a question. He didn't really know what to say but then suddenly he didn't get to say anything.

"There she is," Maggie cried, and they both looked toward her voice and there she came, striding quickly with everybody following her, including a grinning Kurt and his hit television show-making sister.

* * *

"What's going on?" Lilly asked as Maggie reached them.

"The most amazing thing I've ever heard of. And it's all because of Kurt, that awesome cowboy right there. And that's his sister. It's just fantastic."

"Yes, it is." Connie came up and gave her a big hug. "It's going to be amazing—that's the best word for it. I can just see it now."

A grinning Ida walked up and placed her palms on either side of Lilly's face. "It was meant to be. I just can't wait."

As Ida patted her cheek then pulled her hands away,

the talking, grinning ladies parted, and Kurt and the beautiful lady in a very nice blue business suit walked up. Lilly was confused. It was clear that this was someone kin to Kurt, probably his sister; they were both tall and had the same smile.

Lilly had no words. *What was everybody talking about?* Her gaze went from them to Abe, who had a not-so-confused look on his face. But it wasn't a great look; it was a bit of a disturbed look.

"Lilly," Kurt said.

Gus walked to stand beside him and grinned; his gaze shifted to Ida, who still stood there with her, along with her other friends.

Her gaze went back to Kurt. "What's going on?"

The lady reached out and patted her brother's arm. It had to be her brother. "I need to take it from here, if my brother doesn't mind. I am Victoria. My brother videoed an amazing baking class of you, surrounded by all these lovely ladies. It was just fantastic. The ladies were so responsive and you were so very wonderful teaching them, and, well, I couldn't really see their faces because it was videoed from the back of the tent, but just the way they keyed in on you, the way they listened to you and your ability to get them involved in making a wonderful-sounding cake had me from the beginning—well, it had me like from that wonderful movie…" She grinned. "You had me at hello. Why? Because you, Lilly Holloway, are obviously a marvelous chef. But more than that, you have an appealing way with bringing people into a class on what you love. Which is clearly cooking and baking…" She smiled up at her brother, who looked from Lilly down at his sister.

Lilly watched the interaction and it hit her—no, slammed into her. When she baked the other day, Kurt hadn't been talking or reading something on his phone; he had been videoing her class. "Kurt, why?" That's all the words that could come out. *Why had he done that?*

Why had his sister come here? It just didn't make any sense, and her mind boggled, bouncing thoughts.

Kurt cocked his head to the side. "Because I saw how the ladies reacted to you, and, well, I just came in there to watch but I also had been to the inn and I know how good you cook. Believe me, I've eaten your desserts before. Your cooking is incredible but your desserts are superb. So, I couldn't help it…I sent the video to my sister."

"But why? I mean I'm glad you enjoyed my class, but why your sister?"

She stepped up. "Because I am with a major network, and we do real cooking television shows. And he knew we are looking for a new show. My brother knew talent when he saw it. And thank goodness he did. Viewers will be drawn to you. Me, ha, I got the video, and I watched it and knew instantly too. I called a meeting and, well, we would like to have a meeting with you and offer you your own cooking show on our network. We're thinking of calling it anything you want but we think *Glamping Your Way To A Perfect Meal*…or Dessert…might be a hit."

What… Could this be true? "Wait, it's December, not April Fools'. I'm lost."

Everyone in the group busted out laughing. And then Abe stepped up beside her.

"It's not April Fools', Lilly. This is real. You are astoundingly talented, and we all know it."

She looked at him. "You knew?"

He took a deep breath. "I saw what he was doing. I was conflicted at first, then I thought he had a point. He felt like that if he asked you like I asked him to do, you would automatically say no because you didn't see anything in the prospect of it. And after I talked to him and he really was just thinking about you, thinking about letting his sister see it and if she agreed with what we saw, that it would be your opportunity. Your opportunity to say yes or no. And I told him to do it like he originally was going to do. It has nothing to do with me. I want you to soar, and the last thing I'm going to do is get in your way. I had no idea it would happen so quickly." He glanced at Victoria, who was smiling. Kurt was too.

And inside, her heart swelled as she looked around at all the wonderful smiling faces.

"Okay, I'm not mad. I'm just confused."

"We can make it very clear," Victoria said. "It will be very worth your effort. We want to do this, have you teach your class at glamping camps, and we just think it will be a success. We can do it at an actual camp or create one inside, but I think here, like in the film, would be best. Glampers or wannabes will love it. They'll love *you.*"

Lilly's heart thundered as she thought of what had just opened up for her. She had been living her mother's dream, and she had realized that on the walk in. But standing there, with this miracle in front of her, was unbelievable. This opportunity was a dream she never even thought about until she taught that first class…in her heart of hearts, she knew standing there with all these wonderful ladies looking at her, that those two days baking had been perfect—she could have cooked every day with them because she'd loved teaching them so much.

She met Abe's worried, very worried eyes. Her heart stopped. *He was worried she was upset.*

Unable to stop herself, she lifted her palm and placed it against his cheek. "Don't look so apprehensive." She smiled at him, and then she looked at Victoria. "Thank you for this mind-boggling offer. Can you give me just a little bit and…I need to talk to Abe first."

Victoria smiled, eyes twinkling. "You take your

time. I have already made a reservation at what I hear is the amazing Star Gazer Inn, so I'm going to be here tomorrow and even the next day if I need to be. It's a little added bonus to coming out to make an offer in such a beautiful area. So, you all enjoy yourself. You know where to find me."

Lilly smiled. She really liked Kurt's sister. "Thank you. I'll let you know."

She watched as Victoria reached Kurt, then he gave Lilly a smile before following his sister.

She looked around at all of her friends. "I thank y'all for your excitement, but right now I have a cowboy to talk to."

And then she took silent Abe's hand and led him through the dunes toward the blue waters and the hope that was building inside her.

CHAPTER EIGHTEEN

be followed the woman he loved through the dunes, toward the blue horizon, and prayed hard that what he had feared would be a bad thing if she didn't like it was going to be a miracle that he needed so badly, wanted so much. He said nothing, just followed her and cherished the feel of her hand clasping his as she led the way to the water's edge. When they reached it, she turned and stared up at him. His heart raced—no, stampeded—as he looked into those beautiful golden eyes.

Golden eyes that he loved and hoped the sparkle he saw in them was for him. "I'll hear whatever you want to say…good, bad…everything is in your corner now. All I want for you is your dreams to come true. I want you to have everything in this world that you want, need, and dream of and deserve so very much. And that's all you need to think about, not me."

Her lips bloomed into a smile that soaked through him like warm caramel melting over his throbbing heart. Those golden eyes drilled into him, as his mouth went dry and his breath stopped.

"You know," she said softly. "When I got invited to come out here to this camp, I wasn't sure what a glamping Christmas was made of... I had no idea it would be made of my dreams coming true. Dreams that I hadn't even known were there. But that's what happened to me."

His heart—whoa, boy, his heart charged forward like a herd of stallions. He reined in his emotions and forced his words out calmly, "I'm not going to assume anything until you say it outright."

She stepped close to him. "That night you kissed me, my world did a tumble down a dune I totally hadn't expected. It was way deeper than the one I had fallen down when you first came to my rescue. The kiss dune I realize now is not one I want to be rescued from. I realized, walking back from our talk on the beach—even before this wonderful, miraculous event came true—that I was no longer living my dream but my mom's dream for me. Abe, I don't have to be a top chef anywhere—I even knew that before I got this incredible offer. I just needed time to get my head straight, and let you have time to think too.

"This is a wonderful opportunity, me coming here to this camp and realizing that deep down I don't want to be trapped in the back of a ritzy kitchen with everybody doing what I ask them to do. No, I like my life here. I like making people smile and I want to open a small diner—well, you know classy and small, with really amazing food that's not in competition with my good buddies. But there's room for more than just one awesome restaurant here on Star Gazer Island. And besides that, if I get to do a cooking show, that means there's an opportunity that I have a cowboy of my dreams to come home to every evening. Or to stand there and help me with my show as needed out here at this wonderful, amazing camp. I could never dream anything better than that—" She smiled.

His heart was on a rampage. "What?" he managed.

"Nothing better except adding a baby or two after everything's situated, and after *someone,* I hope loves me enough to ask me to marry him, makes my dream come true."

He was stunned. Had no words. He stood there looking at her, his dream hearing her words, stealing his voice. "I—" he managed then grinned.

She did too. "Need me to show you," she said, then lifted her hand, slipped it behind his neck, and pulled his face down, his lips to hers.

Oh, the glamping we shall do was all he could think of as the woman of his dreams kissed him like he had never been kissed before.

The woman knew how to cook, bake desserts, but in that moment, he found out she also knew how to kiss and he joined in…

Her kiss was like whipped cream with cherries on top, and as he pulled her into his arms and tried to give her as good a kiss as she was giving him, he felt like he was walking on clouds. And he knew all of their dreams and hopes came alive, combined in this moment, and he began smiling against her lips.

Then he couldn't do it anymore; he pulled his lips away. "Will you marry me, please? *Please* marry me."

She laughed, tears glistening in her golden eyes like stars to his heart. "You bet I will."

And then she tugged his lips back to hers and his dreams were not just coming true—they were being created in that moment too. Life was good, great. One dessert after the other was on its way and he planned to enjoy this life, this wife he'd never truly dreamed he'd get. Life was a gift. And he'd never, ever lose sight of that again.

* * *

Six weeks after she had asked Abe to marry her, and he had asked her to marry him, there on that beautiful night on the water, they had been married. Everyone was there. The ladies had come and stayed—some at the camp and some at the inn. Her mom and her own special man, whom she'd married on their special Christmas trip, had come. Lilly had been so thrilled for her mom and her mom for her. Knowing Lilly had found happiness and a place of her own in life had brought a huge smile to her mom's face as she'd spoke the words Lilly would never forget.

"My sweet girl, I wanted your dreams to come true, and you found them. You found *your* dreams, not mine, and it makes me so happy."

Now, standing here those words echoed through Lilly as she smiled at the camera and told all the people watching from home that she hoped they had a great day and enjoyed the dessert they had made with her.

And as she smiled, she finished with, "And join me tomorrow when we make a dessert that dreams are made of…you're going to love it."

And then the cameras went off and she looked out at everyone who had gathered for the first filming of her new food show. Not only was it her mom, Ida, Connie, Maggie, and then all of the ladies she loved from the inn and the Glamping We Shall Do group…it was also

Sophie. The beautiful woman held her new Christmas baby in her lap as her newly walking daughter, Tess, stood beside her along with her handsome husband, Riley.

Behind them and beside them were all of Riley's family, rooting her on with smiles. Oh, what a crowd…what a wonderful crowd in a life she had thought was made up of total disasters. But she now knew that sometimes a disaster kept you from making a horrible mistake and led to a life of beautiful sandy beaches, blue water, and sand dunes that led to love.

It had for her. She couldn't even look back now and think of all the terrible things in her life because those things had built her into who she was, and sent her on this journey to meet the man who walked up to stand beside her in that moment.

Abe slipped his arm around her waist and smiled down at her. "It was wonderful. You were meant for this." He gently kissed her lips as everybody surrounding them clapped. Then they tipped their foreheads together and turned their heads slightly so they could see everybody.

"Thankfully," Abe said, "this isn't on camera, but this is how I feel, so thank y'all for clapping because inside that's what I'm doing too. Some of you will want to disagree with me because you feel the same about your sweet wives, but I am the *luckiest* man in the world."

Then he turned to kiss her again, and all the way through her body to the tips of her toes and radiating from the top of her head was the joy that just being here in his arms sent through her.

Oh, what a wonderful life.

"And I'm so excited to get to go next week and see the rest of your sweet family back at Sunrise Ranch in Dew Drop, Texas."

So many of those brothers, who he claimed and who claimed him, had come to their wedding. They were wonderful, and it was obvious when he greeted them and they greeted him that they were truly brothers. She couldn't wait to see Dew Drop, the town he called home.

Star Gazer Island was her home, and she loved the name because she and Abe sat on the deck of their new home and watched the stars at night. But the way he spoke of Sunrise Ranch and the way he said when he was there he would wake up in the mornings and watch the sunrise and it gave him hope after all the sadness he had lived through sounded wonderful too. He'd overcome his past and become the man he was today. The man she loved.

From where he came, there were more stories of hope and healing that he told her about from the other boys who came through that wonderful place they now called home. And all those who were there now she would get to meet. She couldn't wait to go to the reunion and the party in town.

But most of all, as she leaned her forehead against his chest and hugged him so tightly, she was thankful that they were together.

Together and looking forward to the life that they had in front of them.

Now they would watch the sunrise in the morning

and watch the stars twinkling before they went to bed each night. In each other's arms.

Life…it was made of spice, trauma, some worse than others, but if you got over it, got through it, and looked at the light at the end of the tunnel—either starlight or sunrise—life could be better if you just kept going.

If you kept your hopes up and your heart open until you met up with your destiny.

Just like she had done.

Check out book one in my
Cowboys of Dew Drop Texas series,
UNFORGETTABLE COWBOY

"This is a fast-paced read, with a focus on finding comfort, security and peace with one's past, and. the delightful characters will tug at your heartstrings." *-RT Book Reviews (4.5 stars)*

Welcome to Dew Drop, Texas. A small town full of characters who will make you smile and help heal hearts of those who come to town or become part of Sunrise Ranch—a wonderful place for foster kids to become family...

Everyone is thrilled that vivacious Jolie Sheridan has returned to Sunrise Ranch. Everyone except Morgan McDermott. Eight years ago, Jolie left the ranch—and Morgan—for a successful career as a competitive kayaker. Now after a terrifying accident has sidelined her, his dad has hired her as the teacher for the ranch's foster boys and Morgan is in trouble. He knows he can't risk getting his heart broken again no matter how rampant his heart has started beating again at just the sight of her.

Jolie Sheridan was just a small-town gal with a dream that came true when she became a competitive kayaker. Now she's back on the ranch because she can't bring herself to get back in the water and her heart is hoping that old flame Morgan might welcome her home. Wrong…he's closed off and unforgiving of how she left him behind…but she needs help and he's her only hope.

Yep, Morgan is in trouble, just watching Jolie's gentle ways with the boys opens his eyes to the truth: he's never stopped loving her. But she'll be leaving again—she's the best at what she does so he can't let his guard down even though he knows there's something deeply wrong—he sees it in her eyes and knows it for certain when she passes out in his arms.

Can a "family" of foster boys help give this couple a second chance at love? They see it and they hatch a plan…

Welcome to Dew Drop, Texas—you might not want to leave once you meet the wonderful townsfolk and have lunch at the Spotted Cow Café…

About the Author

Debra Clopton is a USA Today bestselling & International bestselling author who has sold over 3.5 million books. She has published over 81 books under her name and her pen name of Hope Moore.

Under both names she writes clean & wholesome and inspirational, small town romances, especially with cowboys but also loves to sweep readers away with romances set on beautiful beaches surrounded by topaz water and romantic sunsets.

Her books now sell worldwide and are regulars on the Bestseller list in the United States and around the world. Debra is a multiple award-winning author, but of all her awards, it is her reader's praise she values most. If she can make someone smile and forget their worries for a few hours (or days when binge reading one of her series) then she's done her job and her heart is happy. She really loves hearing she kept a reader from doing the dishes or sleeping!

A sixth-generation Texan, Debra lives on a ranch in Texas with her husband surrounded by cattle, deer, very busy squirrels and hole digging wild hogs. She enjoys traveling and spending time with her family.

To check out all of Debra's books visit her website:
www.debraclopton.com

Sign up for my newsletter to get notified
about new books, giveaways, sales, and more!
Go to: www.debraclopton.com/newsletter

Check out her Facebook at:
www.facebook.com/debra.clopton.5

Follow her on Instagram at: debraclopton_author

or contact her at debraclopton@ymail.com